LILY'S WHITE LACE

LILY'S WHITE LACE

•

Carolyn Brown

AVALON BOOKS
NEW YORK

Library of Congress Catalog Card Number: 2001092596
ISBN 0-8034-9495-5

Published by Thomas Bouregy & Co., Inc.
160 Madison Avenue, New York, NY 10016

PRINTED IN THE UNITED STATES OF AMERICA
ON ACID-FREE PAPER
BY HADDON CRAFTSMEN, BLOOMSBURG, PENNSYLVANIA

To Evelyn and Roy Brown
. . . with much love.

Chapter One

Lily leaned forward and peeked around the edge of a partition at the back of the church. She was more nervous than she'd ever been in her entire life, and with very good reason, too. She didn't have enough courage to pick up the train of her bridal dress, throw her bouquet in the trash and never look back as she ran out the front doors of the church. She just couldn't do it. Not this late in the game.

Long tapers set in brass candelabra glittered in the dark of the evening and lit up a shiny brass arch decorated with trailing English ivy and wisteria blossoms. A soft buzz floated among the congregation members as they whispered about the most gorgeous wedding in years in Coffeyville, Kansas. Lily took a deep breath and clutched her father's arm even tighter. He patted it, remembering the day she had told him she'd never, ever marry a wheat farmer. In a few minutes that prophecy would be coming true. Dylan Reeder was a tennis coach and didn't know a plow from a pig's snout, but that didn't matter, as long as he was good to Lily.

The pianist struck the right chord and the groom, a tall blond wearing a white tux who looked like a tanned and muscular Greek god, followed the preacher to the front of the church. A string of seven groomsmen, all dressed in black tuxedos with dark purple bow ties and cummerbunds, followed behind him. They turned on cue as if they were eight little wind-up toys to watch the bridesmaids' procession. A gorgeous, blond-haired beauty dressed in deep purple satin appeared at the back of the church. The shiny material of her dress bounced the flickers from the candles back into the misty eyes of family members and friends. Five more young women paraded slowly down the aisle, and then the maid of honor, dressed in the soft purple of a wisteria blossom, stepped into the center of the doors and strolled toward the front of the church. Finally the moment everyone had waited for arrived. The doors swung open and Lily and her father appeared. The preacher raised his hands dramatically and the congregation stood. Her dress was an original creation of white lace covered satin with a Basque waistline and an extended chapel-length train scattered with hand-sewn pearls. Her ultra curly jet-black hair had been tamed into a bunch of ringlets inside a circlet of pearls which held the fingertip-length veil. Even without her normal brilliant smile, no one was disappointed in the spectacular vision in white lace, satin, and illusion floating down the aisle.

Lily and Dylan would say their vows before witnesses of friends and family and begin their life together. And they'd live happily ever after—the only fitting end to a perfect courtship, a perfect wedding, a perfect couple for all eternity.

"Who gives this woman to be married to this man?" the preacher's big booming voice filled the huge church.

"Her mother and I do," Lily's father spoke up loud and clear.

"You may be seated," the preacher said to the congregation and waited until the shuffling stopped before he started. "Dearly beloved," he intoned, "we are gathered here on this glorious summer evening in the presence of God and these witnesses to unite Lily and Dylan in holy matrimony . . ."

Lily's heart lay broken in a million pieces. She could hardly breathe and her mouth felt like it had just been swabbed out with cotton. She couldn't say her vows when she couldn't even produce enough saliva to swallow. If it weren't for the anger lying like a boiling pot of lava in her chest, she would have been sobbing. And Dylan had the gall to stand in front of a minister and the Almighty, Himself, looking like an angel from the portals of Heaven. No one would ever guess that he was a top-notch, cheating fraud. She wanted to jerk her sweaty hand away from his ultra-cool fingers and slap fire right out of his perfect face.

She couldn't look at him or she might throw her bouquet of drooping wisteria and orchids on the floor, double up her fist, and truly dot his eye. The preacher was saying something about the love chapter in Corinthians when she looked at her bridesmaids all in a row. Marcy, her best friend in college, several of her friends and her maid of honor, Rachel—her only female cousin on her mother's side of the family. She saw Rachel wink at Dylan. Slow, deliberate, and sexy. Lily whirled around just in time to see the corners of his mouth turn up ever so slightly in a slight smile as he quickly returned the wink.

"If there be reason why this couple should not be married, let them speak now or forever hold their peace," the preacher sucked up a lungful of air to go on but as if the fates declared her destiny in the split second of a wink, Lily made her decision. She'd thought she could go through with the ceremony; thought she *had* to do it, until she caught that wink between Dylan and Rachel. Suddenly, she knew that neither pride nor fear were worth it. The preacher shook his head and hung on to the microphone when she reached for it, "Not now, Lily," he whispered softly. "You don't sing your song just yet."

She snatched it out of his hand and faced the congregation, who expected her to break out in beautiful song like she often did in church services. "It's a lovely evening," she looked at her mother on the second pew. "It's been a beautiful day. The most wonderful day of my entire life up until now." Several elderly relatives smiled and nodded. "I would like to thank my parents and all my family for their love and support my whole life up to and including today."

People began to fidget in their seats. They'd been to strange, untraditional weddings recently but never one where the bride sounded like she was about to deliver a speech at a high school graduation ceremony.

"I want to thank my sister-in-law, the florist, who made this church look like a picture from a Southern plantation which is just what I wanted. And another sister-in-law for making this dress which also looks like something from the Deep South." She fought back the tears about to spill out over the dam behind her eyelashes. Dylan wasn't going to see her cry. He might feel the back side of her hand across his gorgeous cheek or she might double up her fist and see how many of his perfect teeth she could knock out but he wasn't about to see her weep.

"What are you doing?" Dylan whispered curtly in her ear. She gave him a look that would have froze the horns off Lucifer himself.

"I also want to thank my family for all their hard work in the reception hall. It's a vision from Heaven and I love it," she said.

"But most of all, I want to thank my cousin, Rachel." She turned and looked directly into her big, blue Winslow eyes. Rachel was every bit as good at acting as Dylan because she smiled sweetly as if expecting laurels to come floating down from the rafters and land at her feet. "With family and friends like her, who needs enemies. Just last night my groom promised her that he would divorce me as soon as we got home from the honeymoon and marry her. I refuse to marry a two-timing rascal who can't be trusted. So, Reverend Crowly, there is someone who objects to this marriage . . . me!"

She handed the microphone to Dylan and walked down the aisle in a fluff of white lace. She held her head high and her back straight. Only Marcy followed her.

"You are naive and stupid." Rachel appeared in the doorway of the dressing room at the church about the time she stepped out of the white lace gown and let it puddle up in a cloud of marshmallow-like froth at her feet. "You have disgraced your whole family. Your mother is out there crying her eyes out, and the caterers want to know what to do with all the food, and people are leaving in droves. Probably to tell their neighbors what a twit you are. Don't you have one bit of care for your family?"

"Don't you come in here saying one word to me." Lily pointed her finger at Rachel. "I might be naive but you're rotten to the core, so don't stand there and preach at me." The diamonds in her engagement ring sparkled when she shook her finger.

"At least I didn't pull off the stunt of the century," Rachel snorted.

"You had better get out of my sight and stay out of it." Lily jerked the ring off and threw it at Rachel. "You can have this. You've already got the man who goes with it. And stay away from me. Besides you should be thanking me instead of pitching a fit. Now you don't have to wait for the legalities of a divorce to have Dylan."

"You are a complete fool," Rachel seethed.

"That's the gospel truth," Lily said. "I have been the grand chump fool of all time. But I'm not anymore, and you better stay out of my sight, girl. And you tell Dylan that he'd better find a hole and stay in it," her voice chilled Rachel to the bottom of her light purple satin shoes.

"What have you done, child?" Her mother stumbled into the room, wringing her hands around her handkerchief until she saw Rachel standing next to Marcy. "How dare you show your face in this room, Rachel. Get out!" Mrs. Winslow pointed toward the door. Pure rage replaced tears instantly. "And don't you ever set foot in my doorway again. You've shown your true colors tonight, and you're nothing but trash."

Rachel stomped out of the room.

"I did the only thing I could do," Lily answered her mother's question. "I'm going to Oklahoma, Momma. You have Marcy's address and phone number in the wedding book things. Don't you dare give it to Dylan. If I have to look at him again, I might shoot him right between the eyes, and you don't want a murder on your conscience."

"This is awful. You poor, poor child. But better now than after you said your vows. Still, how will I ever face my friends? They'll be so full of sticky pity it'll make me upchuck," she said.

"You can face them easier than I could face Dylan tonight in the bridal suite of the hotel." Lily put her arms around her mother's shoulders. "Momma, I'll be fine and I'll call often. Don't worry about me."

"You may not have to shoot him. Your father may do it for you. And Heaven help him if he ever has to face your brothers. It's probably best if you do get out of town. I'll take care of the gossip and returning the gifts, too. This has to be a terrible shock. I'm proud of your courage. I love you. Just come home in one piece."

"Thank you, Momma." Lily kissed her on the forehead and left with Marcy by the back door of the church.

"Take a deep breath," Marcy said fifteen minutes later when they crossed the state line into Oklahoma. "You won't get any Kansas air for a long time."

"Hallelujah. Kansas is not big enough for me and

Dylan Reeder both, so I'm better off getting away from it all. If I'd stayed I'd be spending time in jail for homicide," Lily swore emphatically. Anger still boiled out of her like boiling hot lava erupting from the top of an active volcano.

Marcy wasn't surprised. Once the rage vented itself the tears would come along. They made it to Tulsa before she heard the first sob and reached into the back seat of her old blue Camaro and picked up a box of tissues. She handed the whole box to Lily without saying a word and the weeping began in earnest.

"That sorry scoundrel." Lily blew her nose into a handful of tissues. "Why wasn't he man enough to come tell me how he felt about Rachel? And that . . . that . . . that," she couldn't find a word vile enough for her cousin, "Why didn't she say something? To think he kissed me passionately just before midnight and told me he loved me. Then went straight to her arms." She sobbed until her chest ached.

"I know." Marcy reached across the console and patted Lily's shoulder sympathetically. "But a month in southern Oklahoma will help you forget that lousy skunk. And I really do appreciate you living in my trailer and house sitting for me. Jesse is a sweetheart and he said he'd take care of everything. But Momma and Daddy will be gone, too, and that would be three houses for him to watch right in the middle of a busy season. You'll like Jesse. He's a little old fashioned but he's so sweet even if he is my older brother. I'll call him in the morning before we leave and tell him to stop by and make sure you're all right. By the time a month is up, you'll feel better and Momma and Daddy will be back." Marcy's voice cracked and she cried with Lily. "Now, look what you've made me do! I'm a fine friend. Can't even hold up and be strong for you."

"You *are* a fine friend, Marcy," Lily hiccuped. "Anyone else would have just let me marry him just to save the scandal and then when we got back from the honeymoon and I found out what I got, they would have said, 'Well, I knew it all along. He even cheated on you on the night before your wedding.' No, Marcy, even though it hurt you to tell me, you did the right thing. We did the right thing." She blew her nose loudly.

"I'll worry about leaving you all alone." Marcy's chin quivered. "Maybe you should have stayed in Coffeyville and fought it out with the whole bunch of them. They'll think you tucked your tail between your legs and ran."

"I don't give a royal rat's fanny what they think," Lily snorted. "If I stayed they'd all have me drowning in a pity pool, or telling me what a hateful daughter I was for spoiling everything. Men can make mistakes like that, you know. We're supposed to forgive them since they're weak," she pressed her thumbs into her temples. Her head threatened to blow apart with a stress headache. "But I'll never forgive Dylan or Rachel. And I appreciate the offer of your house. I'll have my emotions straightened out in a month, I promise."

Marcy nodded. Was it just last night she overheard that fatal conversation on the balcony right next to hers in the motel? She'd spent the entire night walking the floor, wishing she'd been in the shower when Dylan and Rachel had their tête-à-tête on the balcony adjoining hers.

"How can you possibly marry her knowing the way I feel?" Marcy heard Rachel whine. "I've loved you forever, and you know it."

"How can I *not* marry her? Things have gone too far for me to back out now. You said you wanted to break it off and play the field, and she was there, Rachel. We looked good together and you weren't ever going to be there for me again. Remember that fight we had. Besides, I sure didn't know you were cousins," Dylan snapped.

"Does she even know about us?"

"Of course not. I didn't even know you were related until a month ago. When she told me her cousin from Tulsa was going to be her maid of honor and said your name, I thought I'd drop dead. I didn't know she even knew you until that minute," Dylan said.

"Well, you had two whole weeks to tell her we were back together," Rachel pouted.

"Oh, Rachel, let's not fight," he evaded the question.

Marcy had blushed bright red and hid her face in her hands so the sky didn't light up in a pink glow. She'd eased back into her room through the open balcony door and told herself that it wasn't one bit of her business.

"Fight, darling? Oh, I don't want to fight," Rachel had said and Marcy heard a loud, sickening kiss. "I just can't stand the thought of you being with her. Promise me when you get home, you'll divorce her."

"I promise," he'd said without a second's hesitation.

Marcy had known that she had no choice but to tell

Lily. If the situation had been reversed and she was the bride, she'd never forgive Lily for keeping that kind of information from her.

"I need to talk to you," Marcy had whispered at the bridesmaids' brunch the next day. The hot chicken casserole and chilled fruit cups were papiermaché in her mouth, and her hands shook as she picked up the dainty little coffee cup.

"Okay," Lily had nodded, "but right now I've got to get to the hairdresser and then I'm having my nails done," she'd leaned down and hugged Marcy. "Just keep track of whatever it is and we'll talk about it this evening while we're getting dressed."

"But . . ." Marcy had protested. "I've got to tell you now. It's very important, Lily."

"See you later," Lily had waved. "Meet me at the church at five."

"You wanted to talk." Lily had been all bubbly when Marcy came through the dressing room door. "Don't tell me you don't like Dylan. Please don't say that. I know he can come off a little bit arrogant, but when you get to know him, you'll see he's sweet and . . ."

"Shhh. The others will be here soon," Marcy had whispered, gathering her courage in a deep breath. "I've got to tell you something and you're not going to like it—or me for being the bearer of bad news." She told her the story.

"Come home with me to Oklahoma, stay in my house a while. Jesse could watch the house, but you need to get away," Marcy had begged when she finished.

Lily had been whiter than the lovely dress hanging

on a hook in the ceiling. "What am I going to do, Marcy? The wedding is set. The guests will be here soon. What am I going to do?"

"I should have made you listen this afternoon or gone to the hairdresser with you, Lily," Marcy had shaken her head miserably. She'd feared her friend would faint in a pile of nervous bones topped with a ragged heart. But Lily had stiffened her back and set her jaw, much like she did just before a track meet when they were both in college. "I guess I know what I have to do, don't I?" she whispered.

"You can not marry him," Marcy said. "You can't go through with this just to keep from disappointing your family and friends. He's awful, just awful."

"I have to," Lily said. "Can't you just see the scandal? Momma would disown me for the disgrace, and Daddy would probably drop with a heart attack after all this expense. To say nothing of all those shower gifts still at the house, waiting to be moved to our apartment next week."

"You can actually marry him tonight, knowing he's going to divorce you next week?" Marcy had asked.

Lily had stepped into her wedding dress and held out her arms for Marcy to button the sleeves. "I have to marry him."

"I'm so sorry." Marcy had bitten her lip to keep from crying.

"Regrets?" Marcy asked Lily sometime after midnight after they'd driven in silence for more than an hour, each lost in their own gut-wrenching memories of the evening.

"None." Lily shook her head. She'd planned right up to the time her father placed her hand in Dylan's that she wouldn't shame her family in front of the whole town. Then she could not force herself to say the vows—promising to love, honor, respect, and share her life with the two-timing devil who'd planned to divorce her as soon as the honeymoon was over. That sly little wink which passed between Dylan and Rachel had put enough steel in her backbone to call off the farce. She couldn't have married Dylan even if the whole congregation had tarred and feathered her and rode her out of town on a rail. Not even if they dragged her to the nearest volcano and sacrificed her to the matrimonial gods or if she would be a spinster for the rest of her life. She'd rather be married to a wheat farmer than spend the rest of her life with Dylan Reeder. And she was never, ever going to marry a farmer.

Lily sniffed one more time as they passed through a little tiny town called Mill Creek. She wasn't going to cry again, she promised herself. It was going to be a long, hot, boring month on a farm in a little podunk town in southern Oklahoma. But she wasn't shedding one more tear for Dylan Reeder. Maybe by the end of the month with nothing but time and space she would have all the jagged pieces of her broken heart glued back together.

Chapter Two

The Freemans arrived at noon to take Jacob and Marcy to the airport in Dallas. Everything was a flurry of last-minute instructions and good-byes. Lily rubbed her sleep-deprived eyes and waved as they hustled out the door. Marcy tossed the keys to her car on the bar separating the kitchen and dining area in her two-bedroom trailer. "The nearest grocery store of any size is in Tishomingo. That's about seven miles to the east after you get to paved road, then another eight back south to town. I'll write as soon as we get to Russia and send postcards, but it might take weeks for them to arrive." She hugged Lily tightly.

As soon as they left, the quiet surrounded her like a tomb and reality hit like a bomb. She was supposed to awaken in Dylan's arms that morning. In a king-sized bed in the bridal suite of the biggest hotel in Tulsa, with a glow in her face so bright she wouldn't even need to apply blush. They'd scheduled a midmorning flight to the Bahamas. After a week-long honeymoon, they would have flown back to Coffeyville to their brand-new apartment. Dylan had private tennis lessons lined up for the summer. She'd have had three months to work on thank-you notes, lay beside the pool, and do all those relaxing things a teacher gets to do in the summer if she doesn't take more classes.

That was the illusive dream of yesterday. Today, reality set its heels and there was no apartment, no pool, no husband, no future. Only this minute with gorgeous sunshine she couldn't even enjoy for the hurt deep down in her soul.

The trailer was a mile back a dirt road off the main road, then another quarter of a mile down a gravel lane which was just two well-worn ruts with grass growing in the middle. When they had driven into the yard late the night before, Marcy pointed down another lane across a cattle guard. "Daddy and Momma live about three-fourths of a mile down that way. It's all the way at the end of the road. They'll be gone to Mexico for mission work after tomorrow, but they'll be home at the end of June or first of July. Jesse lives about a fourth of a mile down and back to the west just a little. He built a new home a while back. Call him if you have any trouble. Remind me to put his number on the bulletin board above the phone."

Lily hadn't reminded her of anything this morning. She had barely opened her swollen eyes and given Marcy a hug before she left. Then she fixed a cup of coffee and turned on the television, but the coffee was just bitter hot water in her mouth and the television a flickering noise that did nothing to blot out the vision of Dylan and Rachel.

At noon she made a ham and cheese sandwich, took one bite, and laid the rest of it down on the bar between the kitchen and living room. She picked up a book and read fifty pages but didn't know a word she'd read or if it was a romance or a serial killer thriller. The mayo on the sandwich turned yellow around the edges, the cheese curled up like it did when it laid in a mousetrap too long. She dumped the food into the trash can and ignored her rumbling stomach.

Sometime in the middle of the afternoon, she pulled her dark hair up in a ponytail, didn't bother with any makeup, and slipped an oversized purple tee-shirt over a pair of faded red, wrinkled shorts. Marcy had said she could help herself to whatever clothing she could find since all she'd brought along was one big suitcase full of bathing suits and honeymoon clothing. The tee-shirt smelled like Marcy's perfume and the shorts were a size too big. If she didn't start eating better she'd be too thin by the end of the month. But so far the only thing that tasted even remotely good was the ice-cold tea.

"Do something other than watch the clock's hands," she scolded herself. Under the kitchen sink she found a bottle of lemony stuff to put in mop water, a can of lemon-fresh dusting spray, and lots of scouring powder. She dived into cleaning the trailer as if her life depended on it being spotless by evening. Dusting, mopping, sweeping, cleaning ceiling fan blades. Anything to keep busy. It worked until dusk when she made herself a glass of iced tea and went out the back door to the deck. Her muscles were tired, but her brain was still numb.

The sun was a bright orange ball setting in the west,

pinks and peaches mixing together to put on a spectacular show for Lily when she unfolded a lawn chair and sat down. She sipped ice-cold tea from a tall glass and watched the first day end. Only twenty-nine more long days, each of them lasting forever, and then maybe the dull ache in her chest would disappear. If it didn't, at least it would have a thirty-day buffer between it and the traumatic events of the previous night.

She drew up her knees and wrapped her arms around her legs as she tried to concentrate on the colors in the sunset. Yellow . . . like the lily-livered devil Dylan was. Pink . . . like the flush on Rachel's face when Lily threw the engagement ring at her. Blue . . . like the feeling in the pit of her heart.

She should drag out her shoes and run all the way to the paved road and back. A good run might make her feel more human. But she hadn't brought anything but sandals and a pair of leather thongs. Just what she needed for a honeymoon in the islands. And goodness knows her size seven foot could never fit into Marcy's size five shoes. She'd have to remedy that tomorrow morning. She'd drive into Tishomingo and buy a pair of good shoes. She'd shop a while and maybe have dinner at a fast food joint and then take in a movie if they had a theater in Tishomingo. She hadn't even thought about asking Marcy what was there. And if there wasn't a place to shop or a movie house of some kind, she could drag out a map and go find one somewhere. Maybe she'd have to drive all the way to Dallas. At least it would take up time, that illusive thing that passed too slowly when the heart hurt so badly. Now if she could just get through another night, she had tomorrow planned. That would take care of day twenty-nine and tomorrow night she'd plan something to eat up the minutes on day twenty-eight. One day at a time. One step, and then another, and another to distance herself from the pain, humiliation, and pure old red-hot anger.

"What in the . . . ?" a masculine voice preceded a downright dirty man around the end of the trailer and Lily jumped, sloshing tea out on her bare legs. She hadn't expected to see or hear another human being until tomorrow afternoon when she went into town to buy enough groceries to last a week.

"Who are you and what are you doing here?" the man shook his finger at her and set his mouth in a firm line that left no doubt he was pretty mad at finding her there.

She frowned right back at him, her eyes barely slits under heavy, dark eyebrows forming a solid line. She'd seen him somewhere before. There was something familiar about the way his dark hair curled around an old straw work hat, worn cocked back on his head at a jaunty angle.

"Who are you?" she countered. He didn't look like a salesman or one of those religious folks who pedaled literature. He looked more like a dirty vagabond. Enough anger was blowing out of his eyes that he could even be an escaped crazy from the nearest insane place. "And what are you doing here?" She stretched to her full five feet, three inches, determined he wouldn't see just how frightened she was.

"This happens to be my sister's house." He motioned with a nod of the head as he took in the grungy way she was dressed, and realized she was actually wearing Marcy's old faded tee-shirt. The girl must have been in the house already, helping herself to whatever she wanted. "And I'm supposed to watch out after it. I don't know where you're running from but this isn't a house for wayward girls. And it's not a free night's lodging. So get on down the road. Find a phone and call your daddy. I'm sure he's worried about you," the man said.

"You're Jesse?" Amazement was written all over her face. "You're Marcy's brother. The one who lives near here, who farms and teaches chemistry at a little ju-co over in Tishomingo? She said she'd call you this morning before she left."

"Well, I was on a tractor before the sun came up. And how'd you know all that about me?" He eyed her closely. All that unruly black hair tied up in a ponytail made her look about sixteen, but she could be a little older. Maybe she was one of Marcy's students at the college.

"I'm Lily Winslow. We were roommates in college and ran track together a few years ago."

"No, you're not. Lily got married last night. Marcy went to the wedding," he argued.

"No Lily didn't get married last night. She changed her mind at the last minute." Anger or pain or a combination of both was clearly written all over her face.

"Well, what are you doing here?" he asked.

He wasn't such a bad-looking fellow. Never make a woman's heart flutter like Dylan did, but still he wasn't the bum she'd thought he was at first. The muscles in his arms bulged enough to stretch the fabric of a faded black tee-shirt and he filled out those faded jeans very well. A soft bed of black hair peeped out of the top of the shirt, and again, she had the strangest sensation that she'd seen Jesse Freeman somewhere before. Not at a tennis match, though. He didn't look like the kind of man who'd be caught dead in a pair of white tennis shorts.

"I'm house-sitting for a month," she snapped. She dared him to put one foot on the bottom step with his cantankerous attitude and smelly body. Even if he was just Marcy's sweet, harmless brother, he was a male, and all of them were as trustworthy as the devil's right-hand man. They might look like lambs but inside they were all just raving wolves, and she didn't care if all that dark hair and brown eyes drew women like bees to a honey pot. They could have him. It would be a blizzard in July before she was ever interested in a man again. And if she ever was, it certainly wouldn't be with a smelly farmer. Not even if he was the only man in the world.

"Oh, I see." His voice wasn't one bit warmer. "Well, sorry to scare you. Marcy didn't tell me she had a house sitter. Last week she was still begging me to stay over here, but I haven't really got time to keep up everything. Be seeing you, Lily Winslow." He disappeared even faster than he had appeared just moments before.

One minute Jesse was all but cussing; the next it was just Lily and the sunset again. No hair curling out around a nasty old straw hat. No sweaty odor wafting across the porch on the evening breeze. Not even a look of pure dislike in his eyes. Just a nod of the head and he was gone. And for a fraction of a second, she wished he would have stayed a while longer. She needed a good, rousting fight with someone. Just anyone she could unleash a fifty-gallon drum of red-hot rage on to get it out of her system.

Chapter Three

Lily awoke to the sound of crickets and tree frogs and for a minute wondered what she was doing back at her folks' farm house. She'd lived in town ever since she graduated from college and started teaching school. Her own little one-bedroom apartment on the second floor with no night noises. She opened her eyes slowly, shook the fuzzy cobwebs from her mind, and remembered that she was in Marcy's trailer. She flopped back on the pillows and sighed. Day twenty-eight had arrived with a concerto of farm noises.

She threw back the covers and padded barefoot down the hall. She would eat breakfast this morning if she had to gag down every bite of food. She wasn't going to starve to death because of Dylan Reeder. He wasn't worth it. She opened the refrigerator to find one more piece of cheese and a apple. No milk, no bread, no orange juice. Just a couple of short bottles of Dr. Pepper which looked downright inviting, but she couldn't live on flavored carbonated water or iced tea forever. There was half a box of Fruit Loops in the pantry and a dozen cans of assorted vegetables.

She poured a bowl full of the cereal and unwrapped the last piece of cheese. Dylan wasn't worth starving over. He wasn't worth the bullet to send him to eternity. It was just that her poor old heart didn't know that yet. But it would. This was just day twenty-eight. By D-Day she'd be whole and fit again. By then she would be ready to go home to Kansas with body, soul, and heart all together in a finely-tuned working mechanism that was ready to face the world. Ready to take it by the horns, look it right in the eye, and dare it to challenge Lily Marie Winslow.

She popped a handful of cereal in her mouth and made herself chew. It left a greasy film on the roof of her mouth but she swallowed and put in more. She needed something to look at or think about other than stale fruit-flavored cereal, so she picked up a note pad from the bar and fished a red pen from her purse.

"Milk," she said aloud as she wrote the word. Bread was next, then she started making a long list of food she intended to cook and make herself eat the next week.

She almost smiled when she finished the last morsel of cheese and washed the whole horrid breakfast down with a bottle of Dr. Pepper. The almost-grin disappeared when she opened her suitcase sitting in the middle of the living room floor. There were all the clothes she'd so neatly packed in anticipation of wearing them for Dylan. She picked out a pair of blue walking shorts and a white shirt and jerked them on with shaky hands. She would buy some clothing while she was in town, too. Something that didn't remind her of the weeks and weeks of honeymoon preparations.

She drove with the window down in the old Camaro. The air conditioner only worked at about half speed anyway and she didn't have a single soul to impress, so she didn't care if her hair was a tangled mess when she reached Tishomingo, Oklahoma. She didn't know which way to turn when she reached the red light. Right or left? It didn't really matter. It looked like either way would net about two blocks of town and even if she made the wrong turn, it wouldn't take much gasoline to make a U-turn and go back the other way. She turned west and passed a furniture store on the right, some kind of clothing place and a laundromat on the right. A funeral home, a Dairy Queen, a huge, new-looking court house and a cafe, then a couple of gas stations and she was crossing a bridge over Pennington Creek. No grocery store unless she was going to purchase everything she needed at a get-and-go type place.

She found a place to turn the car around on the other side of the bridge and took a minute to look down the creek. A pretty place with a sand bar and a few people down there swimming. Maybe on day twenty or somewhere in that area, she'd bring a book and a bologna sandwich back to this place and lay beside the water in one of her bikini bathing suits.

The light was red when she reached it again and Lily was glad because as she sat there taking stock of the other end of the town, she noticed a small clothing store. Just on the other side of the light and there was diagonal parking right out front. She whipped into the first available slot and stepped out into the already hot morning.

"May I help you?" a young lady asked when she walked into the store.

"Shoes," Lily said. "I need running shoes."

"Over there," the lady nodded to the right. "Haven't got a lot, but . . ."

"Thank you." Lily said and found exactly what she wanted on the first shelf. Right size, right price. She carried them with her as she prowled through the racks. She picked up two pairs of jean shorts and four men's size large tee-shirts. Blue, orange, red, and black. There was a washer at the trailer and that should keep her clean enough to while away the hours of each day.

"Socks," she said aloud.

"At the back," the lady smiled. "You new in town?"

"First time I've ever been here," Lily said but didn't offer anything else. She picked up a package of white crew socks and added them to the growing pile in her arms. She laid them all on the counter at the front of the store and pulled out her checkbook. "Where's the closest grocery store?"

"Well, Chuck's is the closest. Across the street on the other end of the block, but if you want to buy a big bunch of groceries, you'll probably find it better at Sooner's. Up the street," she pointed to the east. "Couple or three blocks on the right."

"Thank you," Lily said absently.

"Come back and see us," the lady said when she handed Lily the sack.

"Thank you." Lily tried to smile but it didn't work. Maybe by the time she brought her sandwich to the

Pennington Creek sand bar she would come back in the store and shop for something else. Maybe she could even force a smile by then. But day twenty-eight was just too early to make her face do that kind of thing. It was the day she made her mouth chew and her stomach digest cheese and cereal. Chewing and smiling both were too much to expect for one day.

Petunias, marigolds, periwinkles, even a few little containers of geraniums were under a bright striped awning at the front of the store. Not exactly bougainvillea and tropical blossoms, but they still reminded her of the brochures she and Dylan pored over as they planned their honeymoon. She set her jaw and fought a legion of memories as she tried desperately to think about something else. After all, it had been two days and it was time to pull herself up out of the mire and get on with life. To be sure, he or Rachel wouldn't be sitting around moping about the fact they wouldn't have to wait for a divorce so they could get married. Maybe she should have just handed Rachel her bouquet and told the preacher to marry them. At least the cake and food wouldn't have been wasted.

A lonely tear found its way to her eyelash, but she wiped it away quickly. "I'm not shedding another tear for him or what might have been," she whispered stoically.

She stepped on the rubber mat and the door to the grocery store opened for her. She reached for a cart and took her list from the outside pocket of her purse. Bananas were on sale. She picked up half a dozen. Maybe she'd make a pudding this week and force herself to eat the whole thing. She took her time in the store and methodically crossed off each item from her list as she put it in the cart.

The checker asked for identification when she wrote an out-of-state check, but that was all the conversation that passed between them. She heard another checker asking about a customer's new grandchild and all the right noises were made when the gray-haired woman produced a new picture. It was a small town and everybody knew everyone else, apparently. But Lily wasn't part of it.

"Which car?" the young boy who wheeled her groceries out of the store for her asked. "Hot day ain't it?"

"Yes it is. The blue Camaro." She pointed across the lot.

"That's Marcy Shipman's car." He cut his eyes around at her. "I know it by the tag. Only person in the whole United States who would have a vanity plate made with Russian on it."

"Yes, it is," Lily said. "I'm house-sitting for her and she let me use the car."

"That's right. She's off for the summer," the kid said as he put the food in the back seat. "Well, have a nice day, ma'am."

Sure, Lily thought. Day twenty-eight could not be a nice day. It couldn't even be a tolerable day. But maybe next week when she came back to the store it would at least be a decent day.

She unloaded sack after sack of groceries. Too much for one person to eat in a month, much less a week. But even if she gained fifty pounds, she was going to make herself eat every day. Dylan was not going to destroy her body as well as her heart and soul. In a few minutes she had it all put away and checked the clock. Noon. She'd managed to use up half a day and now it was time to eat again. She remembered that she'd planned on seeing a movie and eating at a fast food joint.

"Oh, well, evidently this is just the day to shop and come home," she told herself. "And talk to myself. By the time I get back to civilization I'll be so happy to see people, Dylan won't even matter."

She opened a can of noodle soup and took out a package of crackers. She put a place mat on the table along with a cloth napkin she found in a drawer when she was looking for something to devour for breakfast and sat down to eat alone. She bowed her head for grace but didn't know what to say. *Thank you, Father, for this day.* No, that wouldn't do at all. How could she honestly give thanks for the day when it only brought heartache. *Thank you for the food.* That sounded honest enough, so she said that silently.

The first bite was so hot it scalded her mouth, but it tasted good. *Progress*, she thought and scooped up another spoonful. She stopped to blow it gently. The warmth felt good in her stomach, but then it was so deprived even a botulism-infected bowl of beans would probably feel good. Two days with only a few bites of food and two gallons of iced tea made her stomach appreciate anything at all.

She heard a tractor in the distance. Probably Jesse, Marcy's old-fashioned, farmer brother who wore his hat cocked back on his head and looked like someone she knew from the past. It didn't sound like it was so very far away and any minute dust would begin to filter in her spotless trailer house.

She finished the soup in a hurry and chased it with a glass of milk, then hurriedly began shutting the windows in the trailer. When she reached the one behind the sofa in the living room she could see the dust boiling in the field across the road. He drove a green John Deere tractor. It reminded her of the farm she grew up on. That green color was what put her in the teaching career. If she never saw another tractor or another dusty wheat field in her life, it would be too soon. She slammed the window down, shutting out the drone of the tractor motor and the vision of it making its way up and down the land. She flipped the air-conditioning switch in the hallway to cool and pushed the lever back until it clicked.

She picked up the telephone and dialed her mother's number but hung up before it rang. There wasn't anything to say. Not yet. And just the sound of June's voice would probably make her go all maudlin and start to cry again. She'd erased that one errant little tear this morning in short order. That was progress. She wasn't going to invite a step backwards. She'd call tomorrow on day twenty-seven.

The noise outside stopped and she peeked out the window to see Jesse Freeman walking toward an old truck at the edge of the field. He wiped his brow with the back of his forearm and fanned with that abominable hat he'd had on when he rounded the back side of the trailer. She'd heard Marcy sing his praises lots of times when they were in college together and even when she wrote her once-a-month-keep-in-touch letter to Lily through the years. Somehow Lily had expected someone ten feet tall and riding a snow-white horse, the way Marcy talked. Not a six-foot cowboy/farmer/chemistry teacher.

Chapter Four

Three days later she began reading another romance novel she found on the top shelf of the bookcase. It was about a blue-blooded spoiled lady who had been kidnapped and carried away by a dark-haired, rogue pirate. The man on the front cover had a nose like Marcy's brother, Jesse. She tried again to remember where she'd seen him. Maybe he'd been in the stands during a track meet when she and Marcy ran.

It wasn't at a track meet where she'd seen Jesse Freeman. She laid the book down and visualized Jesse in a little restaurant on Main Street in Coffeyville. Just a leftover from another decade where they made the best hamburgers in the state and served them up on red and white oil cloth-covered tables.

That's where she'd seen Jesse Freeman.

Not in the flesh, blood, and bone. Just a couple of pictures of someone who looked a lot like him. On one wall he was sitting on a bar stool beside Marilyn

Monroe. The other was a picture of him advertising something called Kist soda for only five cents a bottle. Her mother told her he was the heartthrob of her teen-age years. What was his name? James Dean, that's who it was. The nose was the same, the brooding look, the sexy, pouting mouth and that chin. He was a ringer for Mr. Dean, only with darker hair. Even the way he wore his hat cocked back on his head looked the same.

She opened the book to the first page. She'd read three other novels. One a day. All with happy ever after endings. Well, life sure didn't turn out that way and people who thought it did had cow chips for brains. But reading had helped her get through seventy-two hours. She was all the way up to day twenty-five and food didn't taste like sawdust stuck together with overcooked oatmeal anymore.

She laid the romance book down, swatted a mosquito the size of a buzzard, and smeared some more sunblock on her stomach. She pulled back the edge of her bikini and sure enough there was a faint tan line beginning. Dylan had said more than once that she looked like she'd been soaked in buttermilk with her ultra-white skin. She'd show him. The next time he bumped into her in one of the stores in Coffeyville she'd look like an Indian. And by the time she gave that cheating rascal a piece of her mind, he would feel like he'd been scalped by a whole tribe of hostile Indians.

She sighed and picked up her book again. After this one she was going to read some of those serial killer things on the next shelf down from the romance books. Maybe she'd find an ingenious way to make Dylan wish he was dead. A tea made from the dried leaves of one of Marcy's foxglove plants. Dry the leaves, mix them with a drop or two of peppermint oil, and offer it to him as a truce when he came begging on his knees for her forgiveness.

Even that didn't produce the faintest semblance of a grin.

"Evening." Jesse startled her. How that man could sneak up on her two times in just three days was just plain aggravating.

"Not yet," she snipped and shut her eyes. "Afternoon, maybe, but not evening."

"Well, excuuuuse me," he looked down from under the brim of that ratty, old work hat. "Got anything cold to drink in the fridge?"

Her eyes snapped open. "There's Dr. Pepper and iced tea, but I didn't buy either one for you," she answered and sniffed the air. Yes, he smelled just like a sweaty man. Not totally unlike Dylan after a hard tennis match. But Dylan had never had dust mixed in the trickles running down his cheeks or pure old dirt settling down into the grooves in his neck.

"Marcy usually keeps Dr. Pepper. Can I get you one? It's hot for late May. Looks like we're in for a scorcher." He ignored her rude comment and took the steps two at a time up to the front door.

"No thank you," she said flatly and flipped over on her back. She held the book up above her head as she tanned the front half of her body. If he could be rude enough to help himself to something to drink after she'd told him he wasn't welcome to it, then she could be just as impolite and ignore him. She didn't take on the job of baby-sitting an older brother, along with house-sitting, anyway.

Jesse checked the refrigerator—well stocked. He glanced around the house and found it cleaner than it ever had been when Jacob and Marcy were home. There was a roast or something that smelled good in the oven and a chocolate layer cake under the glass dome on the cabinet. He grabbed a quart jar from the cabinet, filled it with iced tea, and went back outside. He pulled a big red bandanna handkerchief from his back pocket and wiped the sweat from his forehead before he tilted the jar back and enjoyed the cool liquid trickling down his throat.

"What're you going to do all summer?" he asked.

"Nothing," she said shortly. "Absolutely nothing! And if I was doing something other than trying to read this fascinating book, it wouldn't be any of your business. What have you been doing all day?"

"Plowing," he said simply. "School starts back next week, and I'm teaching a summer crash course in chemistry so I've got to get my plowing done this week. You got any education in how to run a tractor?"

"More than I want," she said. "Grew up on a wheat farm. I usually just cooked for the harvest crew, but when help was short I drove a tractor or a hay truck—whatever needed to be done. But I started teaching to get away from that. And I'm never, ever getting on a tractor again."

"Got enough roast in that oven for two folks?" He gave her a big, even-toothed grin as he wiped away a layer of dirt and sweat from his forehead.

"Pushy, ain't you?" She was amazed at his rudeness.

"Nope, just hungry. Momma and Dad left a couple

of days ago. I can either be pushy, hungry, or eat a cold bologna sandwich for supper," he said.

"There's enough roast to feed a whole family and you are not invited to supper." She used her forefinger to pull her sunglasses down and roll her eyes at him.

"I'll be here at suppertime with a big appetite. By the way, this is good tea. If I help you with the dishes will you run a second tractor for me until dark?" He stood up and brushed off the seat of his jeans.

"Sure, when they have a keg party at the Pearly Gates," she snapped as he disappeared around the end of the trailer. Whistling as he went. How irritating and rude.

He might draw up a chair and eat at her table but he could whistle until his throat was as dry as dust before she'd park her fanny on a tractor seat until bedtime. That was what put her in college in the first place. She could still remember the day she told her father she'd plowed her last field, and told her mother she'd cooked the last meal for a harvest crew.

"What are you going to do at the college?" her father had asked that hot summer day eight years ago.

"I'm going to run track and I'm going to learn to do something where I don't have to get filthy," she had said.

"There's worse jobs. I'd think sitting in a tractor and snorting dust would be a picnic compared to trying to teach a bunch of lazy girls in this day and age. Most of them don't have the discipline to run out to the mailbox, much less to really run track like you do," her dad had said.

"I love it, Daddy, and I want to be a track coach.

I'll probably have to coach basketball, too, but I don't mind that either."

"Then go for it, baby." He had nodded with a big smile.

And she had. In four years she had a bachelor's degree, a wall full of medals, and even considered the Olympics. A year later she had a master's degree in education, and a job right there in Coffeyville, doing what she wanted. Head track coach for the high school girls, assistant basketball coach, and taught two hours of physical education a day.

Then she met Dylan Reeder five months ago, and it was a whirlwind romance. He proposed six weeks after their first date, and the wedding plans snowballed. He came from Bartlesville, Oklahoma and taught tennis and football at Independence, Kansas, just a few miles up the road from Coffeyville. It was a courtship made in heaven for a little while, until it turned into a heartache from Hades.

She made a pan of biscuits, cut up a crispy, green salad and topped it with her famous homemade French dressing, then dished up the roast and potatoes. He wouldn't come to supper, not after the way she'd talked to him. No man was that stupid, or hungry.

"Hello." He didn't knock. Lily wondered how many times he had embarrassed himself or Jacob and Marcy with his impetuousness. "Looks like I'm right on time."

"For what?" She took off Marcy's apron and hung it on one of the hooks below a shelf beside the back door.

"Supper. I told you I'd be here. No way you're going to eat all that roast by yourself, or that cake over there either. I'm not going to let the hounds or the cats have the leftovers. I'll wash up and be out in a minute."

"You really are pushy." She took down another plate and opened the silverware drawer.

"Pushy or hungry? Pushy wins out every time, especially when there's a chocolate cake," he threw over his shoulder as he went down the hallway to wash up.

She had just reached for an oven mitt and pulled a pan of hot biscuits from the oven when he was suddenly at her elbow, sniffing the aroma of hot bread over her shoulder and making her want to throw the whole pan in his face. Hadn't anyone ever taught him any manners? Dylan would never have just plowed in and demanded supper. He wouldn't have even shown himself at the door if she'd been as rude to him as she had been to Jesse.

"Smells wonderful, and I'm hungry as a momma wolf with a passel of cubs." He grinned as he pulled up a chair. His hair was combed back in a perfect feather cut, only a little longer than it should be at the nape of his neck. His face was washed even if she could still see a fleck here and there of the day's dirt still clinging to his chambray shirt.

"That's pretty hungry," she said.

"Yep, been a long day." He grabbed a biscuit off the top of the stack, broke it open with a fork, and crammed it full of butter. He laid it on his plate and pulled out her chair for her. He took his own place and bowed his head. When she didn't say anything, he looked quickly to see if she'd disappeared.

"Sorry, did I offend you? I was waiting for you to

either call on me to say grace or say it yourself. Momma always calls on one of us, and Marcy decides who's saying it when I eat here," he explained, a faint red blush creeping up his neck.

"Please, Jesse, would you do the honors?" she asked around the lump in her throat. Her father insisted on grace before each meal. Dylan thought it was religious folderol and would have none of it except at her parents' house. He'd informed her they had better never ask him to give thanks for dinner. Why should he thank anyone except the people who worked hard to put the food on the table?

Jesse said a simple blessing and before she could hardly raise her head and open her eyes, he bit into the biscuit and rolled his eyes toward the ceiling in appreciation. "If the rest of supper tastes like cream of cow poop soup, I shall not complain. Did you make these biscuits or did you order them from heaven?"

She wanted to smile but it couldn't get out past the hard spot in her heart. "Thank you, I guess," she said. "Salad?" She passed the bowl to his end of the table.

"Yes ma'am." He reached for the bowl. "How much you figure it would cost me to hire you to drive a tractor after supper?"

She shook her head. Even another romance book with fainting heroines and rogue pirates wouldn't bore her enough to get back on a tractor. Besides, there was a movie coming on later she wanted to see and she'd miss it if she was out there on a tractor seat.

"Jesse Freeman, you wouldn't have enough money if you owned all the oil wells in Texas to get me back on a tractor," she told him.

"Oh, well, never hurts to try." He smiled brightly.

"Besides, you probably couldn't keep up with me anyway. I can cover more ground than anybody this side of the Gulf of Mexico and make straighter furrows, too. Marcy hasn't ever beat me in a duel of the John Deeres."

"Oh, she hasn't?" She raised a dark eyebrow.

"Nope, I'm the best there is, bar none, in all of Johnston County. Maybe in all of southern Oklahoma. There's few men and no women around who can out-plow me," he said matter-of-factly.

"I can out-plow you any day of the week. A tractor has no idea if it's being driven by a man or a woman. Besides, I'm the best there is in Kansas and probably all of the whole state of Oklahoma. And I bet I could plow circles around you." She dared him to beat that challenge. Smart-aleck farmer anyway. Just like a man to think because he's bigger that he can outdo a woman any day of the week.

"You're on. What's the stakes?" His eyes glittered.

"Lunch tomorrow. The biggest, greasiest double bacon cheeseburger, giant order of fries, and a chocolate malt at that Dairy Queen I saw on Main Street," she declared.

"You better take your checkbook, darlin', because it don't affect my masculinity one bit to let a woman buy lunch," he laughed.

"I don't think so," she sing-songed. "You better count your pennies tonight, darlin'," she drew out the word in mock southern style. "Because I can plow as good as I can cook. And that's a fact."

"You just going to lay around all summer?" Jesse grinned and changed the subject.

"Probably after I whip your rear end at plowing," she answered. "Why?"

"Just wondered if you'd be interested in a six-week job at the college. Lady who teaches a summer course in health and a couple of phys-ed courses, mainly aerobics, had emergency surgery last night. School needs a replacement but just for the summer. The president said it'll be a hard slot to fill on such short notice and it's not permanent. Just thought you might want to do something other than try to burn up all that pretty white skin like you been doing every day," he smiled. "Got a master's degree?"

"Yes, I do, but what's that got to do with it?"

"Just makes it look good on the books, I suppose. You interested?"

"Maybe." She saw fuller days and faster healing in store and liked the picture.

"You got an appointment tomorrow morning at nine then. Figured if you didn't want to work I could cancel it. Know where the college is?"

"No, I've been to the grocery store, though. Sooner's, I think it was called. And a little clothing shop on Main Street." The roast suddenly tasted wonderful.

"Murray State College is on down the street Sooner's is on. MIT . . . Murray in Tishomingo," he chuckled but she just looked at him with those blank big blue eyes which said it would take more than a joke to make her laugh. "I got to go in tomorrow for a few things. I'll take you if you want. We can talk to the president and if you want the job, then you can probably start on Monday. That's when summer courses begin. You interested?"

"Yes, I am." She put a second helping of salad in her bowl. "But you don't have to take me to the interview, Jesse. Just draw me a simple map on how I get from these woods to the college."

"No need in both of us driving into town. I got to go in anyway." He cocked his head off to one side and reminded her again of the poster in the cafe. "I'll take you. Then I'll do some farming in the afternoon. What happened that you didn't get married? Woman can cook like this, must have been his fault?"

"I don't want to talk about it," she said. "Why don't you have a wife, much as you enjoy good food?" she asked just as impolitely as he had been.

"Momma cooks for me when she's home and Marcy when she's not. Don't need a woman to tell me what to do, where to go, and how to act when I get there. I'm a self-proclaimed, lifelong bachelor. I like my life just the way it is and sure don't intend to clutter it up with a whining woman. No offense intended." He expected to see daggers flying from her eyes but instead she nodded.

"I see. Well, I may never get married either," she said.

"You going to tell me why you didn't get married?"

"No, I am not. And I'm sure not interested in another relationship for a long, long time. We've got chocolate cake and ice cream for dessert, and then I'll show you who can plow the straightest furrow."

Chapter Five

"Step right up here and order a half an Angus bull and a truckload of potatoes and I'll dig down deep in this poor man's pockets," Jesse grinned, a bit lopsided.

Lily wondered if James Dean ever smiled like that.

"I'm big enough to know when I've been whooped." He hoped he'd evoke a smile from her but it didn't materialize. Actually, he was so glad for the help the night before, he would have bought her lunch at any restaurant in town. To think a little woman who only came up to his shoulder could take command of a tractor like that. Just wait until his dad came home next month and Jesse told him about the work she'd done. His mother always told him if he found a woman who could keep him happy at the dinner table, he'd better be thinking about a long-term relationship. And his dad said if he could find a woman who knew the gas tank of a John Deere from a credit card, he'd better be thinking about wedding bells. But that was a silly thought. She'd just had some kind of painful relationship which she wouldn't even talk about, and all the women he knew talked about everything. And talked and talked and talked. Besides, he'd told her he was a self-proclaimed, lifelong bachelor—even though he wondered where the words had come from the minute they were out. Someday, he planned to marry if a tall, gorgeous blond angel ever fell off one of the clouds in heaven. He'd clip her wings and they'd produce a house full of sons, and live happily ever after. There was about as much chance of that as a blizzard on Main Street in Tishomingo in July, so he was pretty safe in his declaration of bachelorhood. And besides Lily sure didn't look like an angel who just fallen off a big, fluffy white cloud. She looked like an imp who had to go to the beauty parlor to get her horns, and not her wings, clipped regularly. Other than cooking and plowing, she just flat didn't appeal to him. Too short. Hair too curly. Eyes too light. Never smiled. Not one redeeming quality except for cooking and understanding farming, and that wasn't enough to build a relationship on. Maybe a friendship if she'd ever thaw out and let him be close enough to be her friend, but that's definitely as far as it would go.

"Thank you, sir." She looked up at him seriously, her eyes the light blue of a hot, summer sky in Oklahoma. *That's what's so unusual about her*, he thought and cocked his head off to one side. *Those light eyes do not go with all that black hair. Wonder if she dyes it? Probably not. No one would dye their hair that black. It must be natural.*

"I shall have just exactly what I said when we made

this bet. A double bacon cheeseburger with extra cheese, large fries and a chocolate malt," she said.

"Whooooa," he shook his head. "You didn't mention extra cheese last night. I don't think that's part of the deal."

"How much for the extra cheese?" she asked the girl at the register.

"Quarter," the girl smiled nervously.

Lily fished around in the bottom of her purse until she found a quarter and handed it to Jesse, who pocketed it with another grin.

"Thank you, ma'am," he said and then ordered his own lunch.

"I need to make a trip to the restroom. Too much coffee while I waited on you to finish your interview. Women are so slow," he explained simply. "Pick out a booth and hold this number. They'll call it out when our order is ready."

"They might be," she smarted off right back at him. "But they can sure beat the thunder out of a man when it comes to plowing."

She went to the front of the restaurant and sat down at one of the few empty places. Her stomach growled loudly and she looked at the number on the stub in her hand. She was actually looking forward to a big, greasy cheeseburger with bacon. A week of forcing herself to eat and all she had to do was sit on a tractor seat for an evening and she wanted food. It surely was a crazy mixed-up world. One week she was about to marry a classy tennis coach; the next she's sitting on a tractor. One week she was collecting new fat-free recipes for her fiancé; the next she was cooking for

Jesse who thought there were three food groups—steak, roast, and lasagna.

"Hello." A tall, dark-haired man slid into the seat across the table from her. "You the new phys-ed teacher at the college? Lillian? I just saw you with Jesse up at the counter."

"Not Lillian. Just Lily. Lily Winslow. How'd you know I was the new teacher? I just took the job a few minutes ago," Lily answered, fighting to keep the edge out of her voice. Something about the man rubbed her even worse than Jesse did. Maybe all men in southern Oklahoma were egotistical and full of themselves. The man sitting so close she could smell his overpowering cologne was handsome almost to the point of being pretty, but he looked at her like she was Little Red Riding Hood and he was the big bad wolf.

"This is a small town," he chuckled. "Talk travels fast."

Before Lily could say a word Jesse was pulling up a chair at the end of the booth. "Hi, Blake," he said. "See you've met Lily. She's house-sitting for Marcy. She's also the new summer phys-ed instructor at the college."

"Yes, I met her." Blake smiled. "I was just getting ready to ask her out to dinner next week."

"Oh?" Jesse raised an eyebrow.

"What?" Lily wanted to slap the sly grin right off his face.

"Yes, but you've ruined the mood." Blake grinned at Jesse. "Maybe I'll get a minute alone with her another time."

Not if I see you coming first, Lily thought but she didn't say a word.

"So you got one or two classes this summer?" Jesse asked. "Blake teaches at the college," he explained to Lily.

"Number one hundred and fourteen," a voice called out over the intercom before Blake could answer.

"That's us." Lily handed the stub to Jesse.

"Maybe I'll call next week," Blake said.

"Don't bother," Lily said curtly. "I'm only here for a few weeks, and I'm not interested."

"Hey, I'm not proposing, Lily," he sneered. "I'm just interested in a little dinner and sideline fun afterwards."

"Well, then let's get something straight." She leaned forward until her nose was just an inch from his. "I'm not interested in dinner or sideline fun. Not with you or any other member of your gender."

"Whew," he fanned himself with the back of his hand. "I like sass. Makes the chase even more fun."

Blake was out of the seat when Jesse got back with the food. "Got to run, Jesse. Call me and we'll go eat catfish some evening? Since your sister and momma are gone, you're probably starving for some good cooking."

"Wrong," Jesse laughed. "This woman right here can cook like an angel and let me tell you, she can flat make a tractor do everything but tell me a bedtime story. And this afternoon we're going to tear up some more ground. She bet me last night that she could plow a straighter furrow than me, and I'll be hanged if she didn't make me look like a six-year-old on his first time out. We've got a bet going on who can do the most work this afternoon. Production is what we're interested in, not straight furrows this time. And then she's fixing supper. Lasagna and homemade yeast bread. If I win the bet, she's making a peach cobbler. If she wins, I have to do all the dishes by myself. Either way I win," he said.

Blake glared at Lily.

"Have a nice afternoon." Lily crammed a hot french fry in her mouth. Talk about deflating a tomcat's ego, and Jesse did it all so guilelessly.

Lily pulled on a pair of tight jeans she found in the living room closet where Marcy stored work clothes. She tied a chambray shirt over a gauzy tank top, found a straw hat, and was ready for an afternoon of plowing. Let Jesse think he knew more about farming than she did. She'd cut her teeth on the steering wheel of a John Deere and a winter wheat crop put braces on her teeth when she was going through puberty. She shed her first tears over a love-gone-wrong as she drove a bale loader. Besides, she'd already shown him up when it came to perfection. Production was nothing compared to that.

She tugged on her running shoes which hadn't even been used for jogging one time yet. Tomorrow she would start running in earnest, she promised herself. She'd get up half an hour earlier than usual and begin with thirty minutes. If she didn't do something she'd be huffing and puffing by the end of the first aerobics session on Monday.

Half another day down the drain and it hadn't even been so very unpleasant. The interview went fine and the job sounded easy. She stared at her reflection in the tiny bathroom mirror. The same woman looked back at her who had on her wedding day just the week before.

Tall, handsome Blake seemed quite taken with her. As much as Dylan had the first time they met at a teachers' meeting. He said later that he looked across the room and knew she was the woman he was going to marry. Lily went completely brain dead from that moment until her wedding night.

"He could sweet talk a nun's pantyhose down. More than likely he'd used the same line on Rachel." She eyed the woman looking back at her.

She turned to the left and checked her reflection at that angle. The same blue eyes she had this morning. Kind of blah-looking with no sparkle in them. The same full mouth even if it was serious and refused to grin anymore. The same small features which made her look like a sixteen-year-old teeny bopper if she didn't put her makeup on every morning.

There must be something there. Something that drew a man's eye in the beginning and then turned him off stone cold after a few weeks. Blake had that lean and hungry look about him. A tomcat on the prowl who'd just found a new female feline on the block. All she would have had to do was blink her lashes a couple of times and he would have been sniffing around the trailer door by dark that very night.

"Hey, you ready?" Jesse walked in the back door just like he did the night before.

"Just about," she called down the hall. She looked one more time. It had to be there and she couldn't see it. Maybe they just liked the chase as Blake mentioned. In the beginning she had been brassy, sassy, and full of spit and vinegar with Dylan. When she gave in and let him catch her, the game was over. She was tame. And he lost all interest. Were all men like that?

"It don't matter," she whispered. And it didn't, because she wasn't falling in love or even dating again until Lucifer sold snow cones inside the gates of Hades.

"Lily?" Jesse called out.

"I'm tying my shoes. Get ready to lose," she told him when she reached the living room. He wore faded jeans and a tee-shirt with the sleeves cut out. Both looked clean and soft and there weren't even any dirt circles around the neck of the shirt yet or sweat stains on the backside of his jeans.

He was sitting on the sofa with the remote control in his hand as he flicked through the channels on the television set. When he found the Country Music Television station, he stopped and watched Shania Twain strut her stuff. He pretended that he didn't even know Lily was in the room. But Jesse knew the minute she left the bedroom. Inhaled that wonderful perfume she wore as she walked up the hall, and used up every bit of his willpower keeping his eyes focused on the television set.

If only she was a tall classy blond, he would definitely ask her out himself. But after that cold look she gave Blake, he wasn't about to evoke that kind of anger intentionally. He wished to goodness his sister had at least filled him in on a little bit of the reason Lily called off the wedding at the last minute. He'd been on some kind of crazy emotional bungee jump ever since he turned the corner that day and found her sitting on Marcy's back porch. She was the exact opposite of what attracted him but he was drawn to the girl, and be hanged if he could understand a bit of the confusion.

"You going to ogle Shania all evening or are we going to plow?" she asked testily.

"Oh, I was just getting my testosterone fix so I could beat you soundly," he chuckled and she frowned.

"You better get all the help you can, buster," she snipped.

"Whew, little sassy aren't you?" he asked.

"No, Jesse Freeman, I'm not a little sassy," she snorted. "I'm a lot sassy and I fully well intend to stay that way. Cold sassy Lily who has no warm blood in her and who will never wear a flea collar again."

"Flea collar?" he asked.

"You know, like a tame little house kitten. I'm cold, sassy, and that's the way I'm staying."

"You can say that again." Jesse hit the power button and turned off the television. "Bet you won't even feel remorse if I have to do dishes."

"You got that right," she said on her way out the door.

Chapter Six

She wiggled her bottom down into the seat of the tractor and put the earphones of a cassette player across the top of her head. Time went faster if she listened to her favorite country music. She started off with Dolly Parton singing about a woman being an eagle when she flies and wondered if she'd ever feel like flying again.

"Yes, I will," she declared with determination as she revved up the motor of the green tractor. "And it won't be long, either." She checked her watch. Thirty more seconds. She looked at the green tractor right next to the one she drove. Jesse gave her a thumbs-up sign and the two of them were off in a race to see who could get their acreage tilled before suppertime.

Lily listened to the music and did what came naturally on the tractor. Even though it had been several years since her dad could talk her into helping out, she hadn't forgotten a single time-saving motion as she got to the far side of her share of the acreage and turned the rig around. Then Dolly started singing a song about the best woman winning. Well, evidently Rachel was the best woman because she sure as thunder won the battle on Lily's wedding night, and the night before that, too.

Does Jesse have a woman? she wondered. Well, if he did have a woman, that just made Lily all the happier. She could pick up his dirty socks, listen to him moan and groan when his crops failed, and help him grade chemistry papers until midnight. All that interested Lily was a little dinner conversation and a game of wills when it came to farming—and that's all that would ever interest her. After six weeks of summer classes she'd go on home to Kansas and his woman could do whatever she wanted with Jesse Freeman. Just because Dylan was a cheat and a rapscallion didn't mean she was going back on her word about never marrying or even dating a farmer. No siree! She'd find another man who didn't know a bull from a brush hog—if she ever decided to get married. She might just be the old maid aunt in the family.

The dirt swirled up in red clouds and she remembered why she hated this job. Challenge or not, if she had a lick of common sense she'd stop the green monster, declare him the winner by default, and go to the trailer. The soothing power of a long, hot bath tantalized her but she didn't even brake. She'd show Jesse Freeman who was the best farmer and then she'd refuse to plow again, or do anything else that had even the faintest smell of dirt to it.

The music stopped. She fished around in her shirt pocket for another tape and deftly replaced the one in the mini-tape player attached to her belt loop, but she didn't let up even a little bit on the gas pedal. No, she wouldn't give him the satisfaction of winning. Not even by default. She'd work until the job was done and he could get ready for dishpan hands. She would laze back on the big, overstuffed navy and hunter green plaid couch in Marcy's living room, and watch CMT on television while he did the dishes and she wouldn't waste one minute of pity for poor old Jesse. And she hoped Marty Stewart with his tight-fitting blue jeans was the featured artist of the evening.

Dylan would lay a golden egg if he saw her sitting up here on this tractor. *Who cares?* that little inner voice asked. *No one,* she argued back with it. *I don't care what he thinks and I was crazy to ever let him dictate to me how I thought or felt. It was the desire of the moment. It was the whirlwind of it all. He was so good-looking and he said he loved me*, she argued with the voice.

Dream come true, was it? her conscience argued right back. *Be honest, you let him lead you around like a puppy dog on a leash.*

"Shut up," she said out loud. "I don't need this. I've got a field to plow."

But in the solitude on the tractor she remembered the times when Dylan did things she didn't appreciate. Like despising grace at the table. Like the time he had wanted her to trade her clear contacts in for brown ones. Rachel's eyes were blue, too, but maybe she'd already rushed right out and bought brown contacts to please him. That old familiar pain grabbed her heart and squeezed hard when she thought about him being with Rachel the night before the wedding. When she had called her mother the night before to tell her she had the opportunity of a summer job, Mrs. Winslow told her that Dylan hadn't been seen in Coffeyville since the night of the wedding.

"I'll see him again," Lily declared as she plowed. "And when I do, I'll deliver him a speech to fry his brain," she vowed with vengeance. "And that's a promise. I don't care if it's ten years from now and he's got eight kids with Rachel and a beer gut. Someday I'll have my say-so. And if that wench thinks she can keep him, then power to her. The first skirt that flits past will entice him right out of her bed, too. If she can steal him from me, then someone can steal him from her. I'm just a lucky girl I found out when I did . . . even if my foolish heart doesn't know that yet."

Lily put the final touches on the peach cobbler after they ate lasagna. She might be able to plow a straighter furrow, but Jesse beat her fair and square when it came to production. His acreage was plowed fifteen minutes before she had finished and found him sitting on the ground next to the front tire of his rig.

"Cobbler." He had rubbed his grumbling stomach.

After supper was finished, she began paying off her bet. She laid the long skinny fingers of pie dough first one way and then the other, making a perfect latticework across the top of the deep-dish pie. He watched from the other side of the bar, leaning on it with his elbows and not taking his green eyes from the show for even a minute.

"Lasagna was good. Bread was delicious. But that thing is the prettiest piece of artwork I've ever seen.

I can appreciate good ballet, good oil paintings, good music, even good sculpture, but it's going to be a shame to cut into that. Not that I'm above doing it," he laughed.

"Momma says the way to a man's heart is through his stomach," she said.

"You must not have ever made a cobbler for that fool who dumped you at the altar. Evidently he never ate your biscuits, either. If he did, he's a complete idiot," Jesse fished for information.

"I told you, I don't want to talk about it. But he didn't dump me at the altar, Jesse. I was the one who decided I couldn't be married to him, at the very last minute." She opened the oven door, squinted her eyes against the blast of heat, and shoved the pie in on the top rack. "Go get a shower and come back in an hour and we'll have hot cobbler and ice cream for dessert. I'll get this kitchen cleaned up and grab a quick shower myself."

"We'll watch a movie while we eat. Marcy and Jacob have a few of the oldies in there under the VCR," he said.

"No, we will not. You can eat your pie and ice cream because you won and I don't reneg on my bets but we're not watching a movie. I'm going to curl up in bed with a good book." She tilted her chin down and looked up at him through furrowed brows.

"Back in a few minutes," he said. The stupid fellow who got stranded at the altar must have really made her angry.

She loaded the dishwasher while he was gone. She had heated the lasagna in the microwave and had pulled the chilled salad from the refrigerator, along with yeast rolls she'd made the night before. By the time the rolls were cooked, their hands and faces were at least reasonably clean. The last time she ate with such gusto was the year before she went to college, the last year she helped with the harvest crew.

When Jesse had cut a second big slab of pasta from the pan and helped himself to two more rolls, she wondered how he kept from weighing three hundred pounds. Still yet, it was good to see a man work hard and enjoy his food. Dylan had been partial to salads and the white meat of either turkey or chicken. He also liked tofu, yogurt, and lots of fruit juice, and he hated it when she ate a fat-filled greasy hamburger or drank real Dr. Pepper instead of diet.

She shook her head, trying to clear the thoughts of him that kept creeping in every time she did anything. How on earth a vision of him popped up when she was plowing was a complete puzzle. And why, oh why, did he filter into the space between her and Jesse while they ate supper in their dusty jeans and sweat-stained shirts?

Nothing made sense. She'd come to southern Oklahoma to sit and do absolutely nothing for a whole month while her frayed nerves mended. And now she was teaching six weeks of the summer at a ju-co and cooking supper for a man—after she'd plowed all afternoon for him. Just where did the rude Jesse fit into her emotions that had begun to look more and more like a patchwork quilt? He was the exact opposite of the type of man who would appeal to her. She liked tall blond men with brown eyes. Men without a farmer's tan, with perfectly manicured fingernails, and who hated farming. Jesse Freeman bordered on being too brassy and rude to even fit into her mold for a friend, yet she found herself looking forward to the bantering and time she spent with him.

She dropped her dirty clothes in a pile in the bathroom floor and crawled into the tiny shower. She lathered up her hair and then washed all the dirt from her body. There was enough under her arms to plant a turnip bed, and to at least make a flowerbed on her ankles when she peeled off her sweaty socks. Then she rinsed the soap from her dark hair and let it do what it liked to do best, spring up in tight little curls from her scalp all the way down to her shoulders. She put on the thick white terry robe she had packed for the honeymoon with her new initials engraved on the lapel. LMR for Lily Marie Reeder. Tomorrow she would sit down with a pair of scissors and pick every single one of the threads out, or else set fire to the robe and do a war dance around it while it burned.

"Hello." He startled her when she padded out of the bathroom to check the cobbler. "Pie smells delicious." His heart froze in the middle of a beat when he looked up at her. Her bare legs and feet were sticking out from the bottom of the long robe. Several dark curls had already escaped the towel wrapped around her hair. There had never been a woman who made his mouth go dry, and he'd already given her his song and dance about being a self-proclaimed, lifelong bachelor. No one had ever made him hold his breath until his chest ached . . . not once. Confusion filled him. He wasn't a sixteen-year-old kid who got an itch in his underwear every time a pretty girl walked past him. Lily was Marcy's friend and she'd already let him know she didn't want any relationships of any kind at this point in her life. Besides, she had an sassy attitude he couldn't abide and she had curly hair, which he'd never liked. His crazy old heart could just shift into reverse gear and get over its infatuation. He'd been too long on the tractor and away from women in general. Next week he was going out on a date. And that was a fact.

"Where'd you come from?" She pulled the top of the robe tight and stopped in her tracks. "I didn't hear you come in, and how did you get here so fast?"

"When I drive home, I go around the road, a quarter mile back north and another little piece down my lane. But my lane cuts back toward the west at a pretty sharp angle. So if I walk over here I come through the woods at the back of my house, around the edge of the pond and I'm here in less time than it takes to drive. Marcy and I talked about making a road, but we'd have to cut down too many trees and besides the land gets pretty marshy around that pond, so we never did," he explained but he couldn't take his eyes off her.

"I see. Well, the pie isn't done yet." She blushed at his stare. "I'll go find some shorts and a shirt."

"How about an action film?" He flipped through the boxes under the television. "Marcy likes Mel Gibson. Seen all his stuff?" he yelled down the hallway.

"About sixteen times, and I told you we weren't watching a movie together, Jesse. What do I have to do? Put it in writing and make you sign it in blood? I'm not interested in spending time with anyone. Not even you. No one. Nil. Nada. I just want to be left alone," she said stoically.

"No you don't." He shook his head. "You come

from a farming family and you don't want to be left alone. You'd quit eating and shrivel up and die if you were left alone. Hey, girl, I'm not here to push myself on you. I miss my sister, Marcy, and Jacob, too. And Momma and Dad are gone so you've got me. Now, you want Mel Gibson or not?" he asked.

"I don't think you understand what no means. Just put any one of them in the VCR. At least Marcy and I have very good taste when it comes to men on the screen." She rolled her eyes toward the ceiling, but no answers came floating down from Heaven to tell her how to deal with Jesse Freeman.

"Evidently not," he murmured. Marcy might have good taste in men. After all she married Jacob and he was a fine fellow. But Lily didn't or she would be on her honeymoon, not making cobblers in southern Oklahoma.

"What did you say?" She stopped halfway down the hall.

"I said the pie smells good," he yelled back and chose *Lethal Weapon* from the rack of movies.

"It's still got half an hour before it's done." She appeared in a pair of denim shorts and a black tee-shirt a couple of sizes too big for her. She'd raked her fingers through her curls and pulled the front back with a clip, didn't have a drop of makeup covering a faint trickle of freckles across her nose, and he thought she was beautiful. *Drat it all anyway,* he thought. *I'm not going to think she's cute. I'm not going to think of her as anything other than a kid sister, and that's a promise. So, just plain stop it, heart. You're not going to make me feel sorry for that piece of sassy baggage.*

"Ohhhh," he moaned when he started to stand up from a squatting position.

"Cost you to sit in the tractor seat that long, didn't it?" she said seriously.

"More than you'll ever know," he nodded. "Muscles between my shoulders feel like I've been run over with a combine. I've earned every bite of that cobbler."

"Then take off your shirt and sprawl out here in the floor. I'll get some alcohol and work on those muscles for you," she said.

"You do massages?" he asked in wonder.

"Sure, I got two brothers, both older than me. I learned to rub sore muscles long before I learned to drive a tractor," she said plainly. "Take off that shirt, stretch out on your stomach and put your arms above your head." She twisted the lid off the bottle she'd found in the bathroom medicine cabinet.

She straddled his body and sat down on his hips just like she did her brothers when she rubbed their backs. She didn't hear the quick intake of air or his racing heart as she poured the cold, clear liquid on his muscular back and started to rub in deep circles. "Be still, and I'll get your neck, too," she told him.

"I've died and gone to heaven," he moaned. "Tell St. Peter to let you through the doors to bring me some cobbler after awhile."

"Oh, hush, you're just tired from a long week of plowing." She pushed her fingertips into the muscles around his neck and dug in even deeper, finding two knots of tension.

The only time she tried to rub Dylan like this, he had lasted about two minutes and declared she was too rough. Even the masseuse at the club knew he liked a light rubdown after tennis and never attacked his muscles like they were out to kill him.

Good grief, she thought. *I've got to stop thinking about him every time I breathe.*

Jesse moaned.

"Did I hurt you?" She quit rubbing and straightened up.

"Oh, no!" he protested. "You've got four hours or until eternity dawns, whichever comes first, to quit."

She was a fantastic cook; worked wonders with a tractor on a field; and gave the best massage he ever had. Whoever that ignorant idiot was who let her get away from him was probably kicking himself all the way to the Canadian border right about now.

"Cobbler smells about done." She slapped him soundly on the shoulders, and crawled off his back. "Ice cream on yours?"

"Mmmmm," he muttered.

"I guess that's a yes." She reached for the freezer door.

"Yes, ma'am, it surely is." Jesse sat up and pulled his shirt back over his head. When his sister got home from learning to speak street Russian he intended to give her a solid piece of his mind for not making sure he knew Lily's whole story before she left.

Chapter Seven

"Don't make enough food for me, tonight." Jesse stopped by the gym where her aerobics class was held. "Blake and I have a textbook meeting at one-thirty this afternoon. Then this evening we have a science department curriculum meeting. They usually fix us a sandwich or something or other. Here's the keys to my truck. I'll have Blake bring me home when the meetings are over."

"Have a good time." She wiped the sweat from her forehead with a towel. *Hallelejah! Prayers do get answered!* she thought. Several wonderful hours without him underfoot constantly. She might lay out all afternoon and work on her tan. Thoughts of Dylan's face when he saw her all tanned should have at least brought a little smile.

But it didn't.

A new group of students were on the gym floor by the time Jesse left. She plugged a tape into the cassette. She used aerobics in her physical education classes for the high school girls who weren't athletic. They moaned and groaned but they really liked the way it toned up their bodies. And even though this bunch complained of sore muscles and swore every day they would drop the class as soon as they could crawl to the administration building, they were right back again the next day. She turned up the soundtrack from *Dirty Dancing* and wished she could erase the vision of Jesse's easy smile from her mind.

The sun was broiling hot when she got home that afternoon. She parked the truck in the driveway, hurried into the house, and made herself a leftover roast beef sandwich. She put on her bikini and threw down an old quilt in the yard. By supper she had added at least a degree of brown to her tan. It was really too hot to cook and eat all alone, she rationalized as she put a frozen pizza in the microwave oven. But it wasn't too hot to think.

She took the pizza to the deck and laid it down on the edge of the railing around the red wood deck. A jealous streak chased through her when she thought about Jesse laughing and talking with the faculty. They'd been kind to her but she was just a temporary teacher. She didn't know who was married to whom, who had children, all those inside things that make friends. It was those friendships she envied at that moment. At least that's what she kept telling herself as she nibbled around the edges of a piece of pizza.

"But I don't have any reason to be jealous." She talked to the soft summer breeze blowing her hair away from her face. "He's just going to a faculty meeting. But he could have asked if I wanted to stay and go to the library or something," she pouted and stomped across the deck. "It's just fine for him to invite himself rudely to supper every night, but when he's got a chance to do something else, old Lily takes the back burner. Well, that's a man for you, isn't it?"

Suddenly she smiled. Then she laughed out loud. She'd been careful to avoid any place that randy old tomcat, Blake, might be and here she was pouting because she had to stay home and Jesse was at a meeting with him. She giggled until her face hurt and then started off on another tangent. She got the hiccups and held her sides. "Maybe I should go out with Blake. It might make me feel like a woman again. And Jesse could stay home and eat a cardboard pizza," she continued to talk to herself.

The laughter stopped as suddenly as it began and a boiling hot anger replaced it. She paced the deck from one end to the other, then slammed the door hard enough to rattle the dishes in the cabinets when she went inside the trailer. She put a movie in the VCR, but couldn't keep her mind on the plot. She opened the refrigerator and thought about eating a chunk of coconut cream pie. But it didn't look good, and usually either pie or chocolate would cure the blues any day of the week. It was just as well that Jesse had a date with the pretty boy Blake tonight. She wasn't fit company for a band of angels, let alone a mortal man. She wandered back outside and spent a full minute staring at the trees on the other side of the pond. His house was close enough that she could hear his pickup when he started it up in the mornings and yet she'd never been invited to go there—even though he showed up at her door for supper every night.

Lily didn't know where the anger came from. One minute she was talking to herself. The next she was giggling like some kind of fool and now there was enough rage in her heart to take on the job of a professional hit woman. She'd never had such drastic mood swings in her life.

She pulled on her running shoes. She'd jog around the pond a couple of times, then maybe up the lane to the road, and she'd be too tired to try to make sense of her blazing hormones. Besides there was probably no reasoning to be had anyway. She didn't care where Jesse went or who he spent his time with. He'd never been anything but an absolute pest. So there!

Besides, Jesse Freeman was a farmer. A teacher, yes, but a farmer on the side. And she'd sworn vehemently she would never, ever look twice at a farmer. She didn't care if he farmed wheat, sweet potatoes, or alfalfa to feed his herd of cattle. She didn't want any part of that kind of life. Not even if he was a knight in shining armor who laid down his coat in the mud puddle just so she wouldn't get her new jogging shoes dirty. That vision brought on a hint of a smile. She could just see Jesse doing that. He'd probably tell her she was agile enough to jump over the mud puddle and maybe even want her to give him a piggyback ride while she was at it.

She trotted around the pond one time, and then squinted and tried to see past the trees and pick up a glimpse of a house or a chimney but she couldn't see anything at all. She jogged over to the edge of the trees and found the well-beaten path he used often.

The sun was a bright orange ball falling over the treetops when she took her first step into the woods.

The damp, sweet smell made her nose twitch. It was at least fifteen degrees cooler under the shade of the massive trees than on a trailer's back porch. A squirrel chattered angrily at her from a low tree limb and a cottontailed rabbit scurried away not ten feet from her. "Mercy, I feel like Alice in Wonderland," she laughed and turned around to go back for a final jog around the pond.

"It's none of my business what his place looks like. I'll never come back here again," she talked out loud to herself again. "But I'm not going back to Kansas, wondering what really is on the other side of the woods," she said. "I didn't invite him to my house, so I guess I can go uninvited to his yard. Besides he's not home anyway and won't ever know I've been there."

In a few minutes she came out of the copse into the backyard of a sprawling ranch-style house with a verandah all the way across the back. The house was cedar and rock and had two chimneys, one on each end, so that meant two fireplaces. One probably in the living room and one in his bedroom where he and one of his long list of women lazed in front of a blaze in the winter. Did he like tall blonds or dark-haired beauties? He must have a preference. Probably someone knock-down-dead gorgeous like Shania Twain. The thought tormented her so much, she wanted to kick herself for allowing it to materialize so vividly.

She sat down on the porch swing and gave a push. Her world was crazy and mixed up. It had only been a couple of weeks since Dylan proved himself to be the ogre of the decade and she'd sworn off all men forever. She wasn't interested in any of them. Not even Jesse. The mystery lady could keep him. Maybe he just made up the story about going to a faculty meeting. He might have a woman hanging on him at that very moment. He was a man after all, and she could account for every moment of every day and most evenings of his time since she'd been in Oklahoma. So it had been a while since he'd been with any kind of woman. Blond, brunette, tall, or short. He and Blake were probably out hunting up a new sand-box to play while she watched the sunset from his back porch swing.

Well, maybe he'd find one to steal his heart away and they would even get married before the end of the summer. Whoever he chose would never know what it was like to march down the aisle in a white lace gown and know that her groom was an unfaithful cheat. She'd never know what it was like to stand in a puddle of white lace with her heart broken and bleeding for a lost love that could never be. She wouldn't know because Jesse really was a decent man even if he didn't ever take no for an answer. Whoever he married better appreciate him or Lily swore, as she slapped the chains holding up the swing, that she would come back and haunt that undeserving witch until eternity. Because Jesse Freeman was the best friend she had right then and no one was going to make a fool of him.

She scolded herself for letting her imagination take control. Jesse didn't have any reason whatsoever to lie to her. He was at a faculty meeting. Besides, if he wanted to go out with a woman, that was his business. She'd never even smiled at the man. He probably thought her face was permanently frozen in a sour position.

A big gray cat scared the liver out of her when he jumped up in the swing and settled down in her lap for a nap. "Well, who are you, and where'd you come from? Jesse's been holding out on me. He never mentioned you." She rubbed his ears until he purred himself to sleep. "Bet you could tell me some stories, couldn't you, Mr. Cat," she said. "But I'd better get back through the forest or I might stumble and lose my way. I'm not Little Red Riding Hood. I don't know my way through there so well," she said. She picked him up gently and laid him down on the swing without waking him, snuggled her face down into his soft fur for a good-bye kiss, and took off in a jog across the yard to the trees.

Jesse unsnapped his crisply ironed, white western shirt and threw it on the back of a recliner in the living room as he crossed the room on the way to his bedroom. He was starving to death. Most of the time they at least served sandwiches and chips at the evening meetings, but the lady who was supposed to bring them had some kind of emergency and they were left with nothing but coffee and some hastily rustled up store-bought cookies which tasted like flour and water.

And then there was that incident with Amber. He had been waiting alone in the hallway for the rest of his colleagues when she appeared out of nowhere. She plastered her body up to his side so tight he could feel her heart beating. "How about a little nightcap down at the sand bar at the dam?" she whispered in his ear.

"I'm busy, Amber," he said coldly.

"I remember when you weren't too busy for me," she pouted.

"That was a long time ago," he told her.

"So," she giggled. "We can make up for lost time."

"No thanks." Jesse shook his head. His idea of a fun-filled evening was not drinking and flirting on the banks of the creek like freshmen in college.

He chased the vision of her from his mind as he yanked his leather belt out of the loops of his jeans and threw it on the floor. He picked up a tee-shirt from the edge of his bed and pulled it over his head with a snap. The only thing in his stomach right then was a cup of coffee from the faculty meeting and confusion about Amber. Whatever had made her come on to him at this point anyway? She had barely even had time to say hello when their paths crossed the past ten years.

"Maybe Lily's got a cold biscuit," he muttered as he used the boot jack to get his dress boots off his feet. He slipped on his athletic shoes. "If she hasn't got leftovers, then she might have some of that coconut pie left. At least it would be something in my grumbling gut."

Elvis, his big gray cat, jumped down from the porch swing and met him at the back door. Strange. When he picked the cat up it smelled like Lily's perfume. When he started through the woods, he could see the pie setting on the shelf in the fridge, could almost taste it and hoped Lily could be coerced into maybe making him one of her famous omelets.

There was a full moon but it was still dark in the woods so he didn't see her until his toe actually touched her back. "Lily?" He recognized that oversized tee-shirt with a picture of a cat on the front. He turned her over and warm, sticky blood covered her face. "Good grief!" He felt the vein on her neck for a pulse, then picked her up and started running back toward his house.

Chapter Eight

"Put me down right now," the lifeless bundle in his arms wiggled and declared in a loud, clear voice.

"Lily?" He stopped in his tracks. "You scared me. I thought you were dead."

"It'll take more than a cottontail rabbit to kill me. I'm a little tougher than that but the thing did give me a start and make me stumble." She reached up and touched her bloody forehead when he set her on her feet beside the porch swing. The ground swirled up in a medley of green, black, and brown, but she set her jaw and willed herself to stand upright. She'd never depend on a man again, not to hold her for any reason.

"Let's get you inside and clean up that head. We may need to drive into Tishomingo to the hospital and get a few stitches. Looks like you've had a pretty good fall." Jesse put his arm around her waist for support and led her in the back door into a big country kitchen. She shrugged away from him and walked to the kitchen on her own power, but was very glad to sink into a chair. He hurried back from somewhere down a long hallway and opened a red and white first-aid kit. He poured hydrogen peroxide on a gauze pad and gently dabbed the blood away from her face.

"Head wounds always bleed like a stuck hog," she said, "so don't panic until you see the actual wound. I suppose I've got blood in my hair?"

"Lots of it, but it'll probably dry stiff as a board and you can pretend it's that mousse stuff you girls like," he teased, relieved to find it was just a puncture wound. Even though it was still seeping a little blood, it didn't need stitches. "What made you fall?"

"A stupid rabbit. It darted out in front of me and I swerved to miss him, stepped in a hole and tumbled. I blacked out for a minute and when I woke up you were carrying me," she said. "I couldn't have been out but for a second or two."

"Don't bet on it." Jesse poured alcohol on a clean gauze pad and dabbed the wound.

"Ouch! That burns." She started to put her hand up and he grabbed it and held it tightly as he blew on the sting to cool it. The sensation was almost more than Lily could endure. There was the faint smell of coffee on his breath and his aftershave lotion was still strong enough that every time she inhaled she caught a whiff of something woodsy, sexy, and wonderful.

"It's supposed to burn." he grinned. "What on earth were you doing in the woods at night anyway?"

"I got bored so I took a walk," she said honestly. "The path was there at the edge of the woods, and you've never invited me to your house, so I just walked through the woods, sat on your back porch, loved on your cat which you never told me about, and started home. What time is it?"

"Nine." He looked up at a clock.

"I checked my watch just before I kissed the cat good night. It was quarter to nine so I really did just fall when you came along," she said. "Thanks for taking care of me, Jesse," she said begrudgingly.

"Hey, nothing to it. You should see Marcy when I have to dab a wound with alcohol. You'd think I was torturing her with thumb screws." He snapped the lid shut on the first-aid kit. "I think I better take you home in my old work truck. I'll stay the night on the couch over at the trailer. You might wake up with a horrid headache and need something. And it could be a slight concussion. Hold this tightly against your forehead." He peeled the paper off another gauze pad and handed it to her, "I'll get clothes for tomorrow morning. Bet that thing really smarts when you start jumping around in phys-ed class," he continued as he disappeared down a hallway.

She looked around at the rustic kitchen which opened into a huge living room with a natural stone fireplace covering the whole north end of the room. She could see a doorway into what looked like a small office and another door with a section of the same stone on the floor. Must be the front door leading out to the porch.

"I'll give you the grand tour of my house another day, when you haven't done battle with a big, mean bunny." He noticed her eyeing the house. He had a briefcase in one hand and a garment bag in the other. "I'll put these in the truck and come back for you. Sit still and wait for me. You might be a little woozy for a little while after a fall like that."

"I can walk," she said.

"Lily Winslow, you are the stubbornest, most independent woman I've ever met." He set his jaw.

"Yes, I am." She held her head high. "And that's the way I'm staying. What's the matter? You afraid I'll be too sick to cook your supper tomorrow night?"

"That's exactly what I was afraid of," he snorted. "Not that you'd ever ask me to have supper with you."

"I don't have to ask. You're just there like . . ."

"Like what, Lily?"

"Like . . . oh, hush, I've got a headache and I want to go to bed . . ."

"Is that an offer?" He raised a rakish eyebrow.

"Sure the day that there's a snowstorm in July, Jesse Freeman. So get that look off your face. Besides, you are a lifelong bachelor. I'll take a ride home but you are coming back here for the night. I don't need you," she told him.

"Yeah, right." He followed her out the door. "I'm not about to mess with my meal ticket. I'm staying the night."

It took a lot of determination but she walked from the truck to the trailer when he parked. She'd show him that she didn't need him and he could just chase his happy, smiling face right back across the pasture to his house. "I'm taking a shower. You can go home." She started down the hallway without even looking at him.

"I'll be here all night." He fluffed a throw pillow and stretched out on the sofa. "Good night, Lily. Take a couple of aspirin after your shower," he said.

"You are awful," she snapped.

"Yep, I am." He pointed the remote control at the television and the middle of a weather report filled the room.

She moaned when the hot water hit her shoulder. Tomorrow she'd probably feel like she'd been slung off the back of a wild bronc. But this wasn't the first time she'd had an accident, and it sure wouldn't be the last. Dylan referred to her often as his clumsy country queen.

Rats, she thought. *Am I ever going to shake him completely out of my mind?*

Jesse was quiet as he drove to the college the next morning. Usually he chattered about a new calf or the need for rain for the alfalfa crop. Most likely he had a horrid night since he felt compelled to sleep on the couch. The spare bedroom in the trailer didn't have a bed, just a desk, computer, and lots of books. Dark circles under his normally bright eyes said there was no way he slept well, especially with all six feet of him curled up on a trailer-sized sofa. She made him a working man's breakfast just to show him she was just fine and he'd slept uncomfortably for nothing. He ate as if he hadn't seen food in two days and even bragged on her biscuits and sausage gravy. But then he was quiet the rest of the morning. Apparently she had pushed their budding friendship to the last notch when she took it upon herself to go prowling around his property—uninvited. She had probably hurt his feelings when she told him to go home.

Oh no. She shook her head. She didn't hurt his feelings because it was impossible to hurt Jesse's feelings.

He did what he wanted and to the devil with anyone else.

Jesse had raided the refrigerator at midnight, finishing off the coconut pie and two pieces of barbecued chicken. Then he had laced his hands behind his head and tried to make sense of the dilemma of his life and heart since Lily had moved into his sister's trailer house. He liked sitting down to the table with her and the easy bantering back and forth about who could plow the best and the most. Normally, he liked tall blond women but somehow Lily had gotten under his skin. And no amount of laying awake at night staring at the ceiling seemed to produce any kind of answers to the questions in his heart.

He was deep in thought that morning when they went through Reagan and didn't even remember turning south for the final eight-mile stretch into town. Then suddenly there was the red light in the middle of town. He turned east down Main Street to the next red light and then right to the college. He nosed the white truck into a parking place in front of the gym where she had her classes.

"Lily, it never dawned on me to invite you to my place. I just assumed that you'd come over there any time you wanted. Marcy and the rest of the family don't wait for invitations. We're just family, and I guess I forgot that you aren't a sister just like Marcy." He blushed slightly but she didn't catch it. Looking at Lily and saying the word 'sister' was like a visual oxymoron. Two opposing teams at battle. She'd become his friend in spite of her sassy tongue. Like a true sister, cooking for him, massaging his aching muscles, and enjoying the same action movies he did. But his body didn't think of her a sister, and he longed to reach out and touch the band-aid on her forehead, to gently run his callused hand down the light sprinkling of freckles across her nose. She'd been hurt severely by some kind of clod of a fiancé and didn't want any kind of relationship at this point . . . maybe never with a plain farmer like Jesse.

"Thanks Jesse," she smiled and his heart threw in a couple of double beats. Evidently that's what she wanted to hear all these weeks. That she was just part of the family and he didn't have any intentions of pushing her into some kind of unwanted relationship. He'd done everything for weeks to get her to smile. He'd bantered, teased, made bets, taken her to lunch. They'd argued with a passion. And now, just when he was on the very verge of thinking of something more than a platonic relationship with Lily, she smiled, letting him know that she liked being another sister.

Women! He fought down the impulse to slap the steering wheel.

His sister! she thought. *Well, if that wasn't just what she needed to hear that morning.* She was glad she didn't have to have an invitation to go to his house. By golly, she might just start walking in the back door without even knocking and asking him when supper was going to be finished. But his *sister!*

"How about lunch in the park. Tacos and cokes. On me for your medical services last night," she managed to get out past the rising irritation.

"Love it," he nodded. "Then I'll take you home for a grand tour of my house, and tonight we'll go to Ardmore and eat fish for supper. I've been wanting a big platter of fried catfish for weeks. So tonight I'll show you the best little catfish place in southern Oklahoma," he laughed.

"Okay," she smiled again. So tonight he was taking his "sister" to eat. Somehow it made her mad instead of glad.

She still didn't have the crazy, mixed-up emotions straightened out when she opened the door to the empty locker room. She peeled off her jeans and put on a bright blue leotard and tights to match. She winced as she pulled the terry elastic band over her head and then straightened it up just above the wounded place on her forehead. Amazing, that a hole that little could smart so much when even a soft piece of terry cloth touched it. *Amazing that your heart, no bigger than a saucer, can hurt so bad, too, isn't it?* That smart-aleck voice inside her head said.

Jesse whistled as he parked the pick-up under a big pecan tree. "Want to get out and sit at the table? It's hot and there are flies, but it's fresh air and more elbow room," he said.

"Sure." She picked up the two drinks. "You get the food and napkins. I'm not a very feminine eater when it comes to tacos. I usually have stuff dripping off my elbows by the time I'm finished. But I'm so hungry I could eat an Angus bull, hide, hoofs, and even the pertinence thereof. So lead the way."

She dove into the first taco and wanted ask him outright if he had a permanent girlfriend. She didn't know how to approach it without seeming downright nosy. She'd been house-sitting for three weeks and not one time had he been out on a date. Maybe if she would just ask like a sister—that thought almost made her choke on the tortilla shell, but she managed to get the bite down without spewing.

"So did your head ache in class this morning?" he asked.

"Not so bad. I had a good doctor last night. He poured in some firewater and I think it cauterized every nerve ending all the way to my toenails. The rest of my body is afraid to get sore or hurt, for fear he'll make it hurt like he did the hole in my head," she laughed.

A sincere laugh. The first one Jesse had heard and it made his heart soar. She was mending. It took an accident but she really laughed. A deep-down-in-the-chest giggle that he loved, but he'd be hanged before he let her know how much he enjoyed it.

"Good tacos. But the fish tonight will be even better. The cafe isn't much to look at but the food is scrumptious," he said.

"Oh, I thought it might be a fancy, romantic place," she smiled.

Three smiles in one day. He wanted to jump on the table and do some kind of tap dance. He'd begun to think the pain in her heart would never go away.

"The Fish Place," he chuckled. "Fancy? It's an old house Miss Maude converted into a cafe. It's got rough wood floors, and red oilcloth on the tables. The records on the jukebox are from the '70s and all country because Miss Maude doesn't like any other kind of music. She plays the songs so loud it'll almost deafen you. There's bandannas on the table for napkins and you'll use a couple, maybe three before the night is over because the fish and fries and hushpuppies are greasy. It's not fancy or romantic so don't wear a ball gown or your diamonds."

Lily didn't mind eating at a greasy spoon cafe. She loved fried fish and hushpuppies and hoped they served up a healthy portion of coleslaw and pinto beans with it. She unwrapped another taco and bit into it while she tried to form the words into a question. Finally she simply blurted it out, "Jesse, have you got a girlfriend?"

"Well, what brought that on?" he asked.

"Surely, you don't spend every waking minute with Blake? And he's the only person you ever talk about other than your Mom and Dad, or Marcy and Jacob." She raised an eyebrow.

He set his mouth so firmly that she almost giggled again.

"Are you suggesting that I'm . . ." He frowned.

"No, I'm not. It's just that . . ." She blushed when she realized what he thought she was really asking.

"I love women. I date occasionally. But . . ." How did he tell her that he hadn't wanted to date anyone else from the time he walked around the trailer and found her sitting on the back porch? She'd take it wrong and get that frightened look in her eye just like she did when Blake teased her about asking her out to dinner. Jesse was a patient man and he could wait for her to heal before he made any kind of move. Maybe by then he'd decide he couldn't put up with her sass anyway.

"But, what, Jesse?"

"Nothing," he grinned. "I don't have a woman in my life right now that I date on a steady basis." He chose the words carefully.

And I'm your sister, she thought with a heavy sigh.

Chapter Nine

Lily dragged out the ironing board and pressed a bright floral sundress with spaghetti straps. Huge blue flowers were set in a swirling design of brilliant yellows, greens, and reds. It looked like something from the Pacific Islands and the blue flowers were only a little deeper than her eyes but not any more dazzling. She was supposed to wear this dress when she and Dylan went out for supper the first night of their honeymoon. For the first time since the wedding night, she could actually keep down the fiery anger when she thought about him. He'd never see her in the sundress, never know what it was like to wake up next to her and eat a he-man working man's breakfast which she had prepared. She shut her eyes and gave a brief prayer of thanks that at last her heart had stopped wringing itself into a knot when his name crossed her mind. Now if she could just quit catching her breath in a moment of pain when his vision flitted through her imagination, she would really consider herself making progress.

"Doing much better," she sing-songed with a wide grin lighting up her blue eyes. She pulled the dress up from the bottom, adjusted her strapless bra and wiggled down to make her silk bikini underpants feel better. She picked up a pair of stringy red leather sandals and was tying the lace around her ankle when someone knocked at the door.

No one had ever knocked since she'd been living here. Jesse was the only one who ever came around and he just yelled "hello" and walked right in. Maybe Marcy's parents had come home a couple of days early. She hopped to the door, one shoe on, the other in her hand.

"Hello." Jesse leaned against the doorjamb, looking like a man out of an advertisement on the back of a western catalog. Tight-fitting, starched and creased Wranglers were bunched up over his shiny, black boot tops and his deep green western-cut shirt set off the green flecks in his pecan-colored eyes. She took a deep breath and sucked in a lungful of woodsy aftershave lotion that made her hormones weep in agony.

"Why did you knock?" she asked, amazed that she could find enough air to speak.

"I don't just walk into the house when I'm taking a pretty lady to dinner," he grinned. "Don't you look fabulous, Lily. I love that dress." He wanted to touch her bare shoulder but was afraid he couldn't stop at just one slight brush against the softness of her bare skin against his callused old work hand.

"Well, then *brother* Jesse, let me get this other shoe on and we shall begin our evening. A tour of your home first?" She looked forward to a deviation from the routine.

Brother, he moaned silently. So that's the way she felt. And just when he had finally come to grips with his own emotional upheaval where she was concerned.

"Nope, dinner first. My stomach is about ready to rebel. The tacos are gone, and so is a pint of rocky road ice cream. It is ready for fish and I shall not disappoint it." He opened the door for her.

Just as Jesse had described, The Fish Place was not a romantic paradise. The music was so loud she could hear it when they stepped out of the truck. The exterior was an old house in bad need of a paint job. The porch was strung with fish netting and a young couple sat in the swing, laughing and talking until Jesse and Lily walked up on the porch.

"Got a waiting line?" Jesse asked.

"Nope, plenty of room right now," the young man said. "We're waiting for someone else."

"Great." Jesse held the door for Lily and the inside was bustling but not full.

Jesse chose a table in the far corner. "I want sweet tea," he told the waitress over the top of the noisy jukebox. "Lily?"

"Got Dr. Pepper in bottles?" Lily had her nose in the menu and didn't even look up.

"You bet." The waitress disappeared.

"I love good Dr. Pepper in a bottle." Lily picked it up as soon as lady set it down, tilted it back, and let the icy cold liquid cool her mouth.

"Yep." He did the same with a frosty mug of iced tea. "Ready to order or need to study the menu more? I already know what I want."

"Then order me the same." She laid the menu aside. "You know what's good and I'm starved. Just make sure they put plenty of it on the plate. They got pinto beans with the fish?"

"Beans, coleslaw, hushpuppies, fries . . ." He nodded and waved to the waitress.

"We want two of the all-you-can-eat catfish dinners," he ordered.

"I'm going to eat until I'm sick," she announced.

"I'm not holding your head up and feeling sorry for you if you eat too much," he declared. "I used a lot of my sympathy quota just doctoring up your evil bunny wound last night. You throw up; you clean up."

"You, sir, won't have to hold up my head. It was just a statement about how hungry I am."

"And now Lily," he lowered his head seriously, "I want to know about this fiancé you left standing at the altar. I finally got a letter from Marcy today. She said he was a rascal. But couldn't you have been a little more discreet? To leave a man standing there in front of a whole churchful of people? What did he do so terribly wrong as all that? She wrote that she hoped I'd drop by occasionally and check on you since you were used to a big family around you. She just said he was a scoundrel and deserved being left at the altar and she hoped your brothers tarred and feathered him and rode him out of town on a bed rail. But I cannot imagine what a man could do to make you and Marcy both that mad. What on earth did he do?"

"I told you I don't want to discuss it." She cocked her head to one side and held the cold Dr. Pepper bottle to her cheek.

"But I do." He leaned back in his chair and the pearl

snaps on his shirt strained against the muscles in his chest. "I want to know what a man has to do to make you that mad."

"First, we discuss something else, then." She set the beer bottle down and put her hands in her lap. The song on the jukebox ended abruptly and a deafening silence filled the room for a few seconds. Then the buzz of many people readjusting the volume of their own conversations started. "First we talk about you, Jesse. Why are you still a bachelor at thirty? And what kind of woman is it going to take to make you wait at the front of the church?"

"Why? What has that got to do with anything?"

"I just wondered. You want to know about the man I left standing at the front of the church with a microphone in his hands. I want to know what kind of woman will put you in the same spot," she said. "Show me yours and then I'll show you mine. If you want to know my sad tale of woe then put yours on the table first."

"I want a family someday." He looked right into her eyes. "I told you I was a self-proclaimed lifelong bachelor and I will be until my dying day if I can't find the right woman. You know what Reagan is, Lily. It's not even big enough to be called a dot on the map. If you get out a map of Oklahoma it doesn't even list the population of Reagan and there's towns with populations of less than a hundred listed. There's little or no social life out there. Just living and someday loving. But women today aren't interested in that. They want all kinds of social things. I want a woman who loves me for me. Who'll love me so much she'll move to Reagan and share my house and life and love me. And I've not found one like that."

"But what if she wants some kind of life of her own? Can't she have some social things and live in Reagan, too?" Lily asked.

"Of course. Momma does. She goes into club every month and she's active in the church, too. But she's a farm wife first. And my wife will love me first, be a farm wife next, and then the social things can come in behind that. I love farming and the land. I couldn't even stay away from the smell of dirt when I went to college. They offered me free room and board and I commuted all those miles every day because I wanted to be on my own land. I lived in the trailer Marcy has now while I was in college. I saved enough to buy my house. Mother and Dad gave me and Marcy each five acres for our high school graduation. She traded hers for mine two years ago. She got the trailer in the deal and I got the building site I wanted. I'd never leave my farm. Teaching and farming are my two biggest loves." He chuckled again.

"I see," she said but there wasn't a smile.

"Here's dinner," he changed the subject abruptly when the waitress brought a big tray laden down with food.

"Oh my." Lily eyed enough to feed a harvest crew of a dozen. "Do you think we've got enough?"

"Well, we can always go find a banana split afterwards if you're still hungry." He picked up a hot french fry and popped it into his mouth while the waitress put the plates in front of them and then placed a red plastic basket of hushpuppies and two oversized bowls of beans in the middle of the table.

"Need anything else just snap your fingers," she said.

"Good," she mumbled around a bite of hot, crunchy catfish, fried with a thick coating of cornmeal and just a bit on the hot side. "What's in the corn meal? Tastes hot!"

"Miss Maude believes in using a little cayenne red pepper. Sells a lot of tea that way." He picked up a chunk of fish with his fingers. "Now it's your turn."

"I already tasted the fish." Her blue eyes glittered. "It's the best I ever put in my mouth. Next time I fry catfish, I'm throwing in some red pepper. Betcha my brothers would drink enough tea to float the Titanic."

"Want to go see that movie after we eat?"

"I'd love to." She smiled and dipped into the beans. "Mmmmmm." She shut her eyes. "Miss Maude can come live with me."

"But your fiancé can't, huh, Lily?" he pressured gently for the story.

"No, never." She took a drink of her second Dr. Pepper. "He's not welcome to even let his shadow cross my doorway."

"I'm waiting." Jesse picked up a hushpuppy, broke it in half, and cooled it by tossing it from one hand to the other.

"Okay, I met Dylan at Christmas at a party. He was a tennis coach in Independence, and it was a whirlwind romance. He asked me to marry him six weeks later and I said yes. Then the wedding plans got bigger and bigger and we had about five wedding showers. I guess he didn't think he could back out of it. I'm not making excuses for him. He's lower than a snake's belly. Anyway we had the rehearsal dinner and he kissed me goodnight." She stopped and a stab of jealousy pierced his heart.

"We didn't have enough room to put everyone up at our house, so Daddy rented several rooms at a motel. Marcy and the bridesmaids stayed there. Just so happened Marcy was on the balcony and overheard Dylan and my maid of honor on their balcony right next to hers. They'd dated last year and broke up just about the time I met him. But I didn't know about that or the fact that they'd gotten back together the month before and they had practically been living together the whole month before the wedding. He promised her that as soon as we got home from the honeymoon he'd file for divorce. It hurt Marcy but she had to tell. I thought I couldn't stop the wedding. I mean, there were already guests in the church, Jesse. I could not embarrass my mother and disgrace my dad so I decided to go through with it and then have it quietly and conveniently annulled the next week. But then Dylan looked at Rachel and winked. I wasn't supposed to see it, but I did, and it was the straw that broke the camel's back. So I just took the microphone out of the preacher's hand when he asked if there was anyone there who thought the wedding shouldn't take place. I thanked my folks for their support, my sister-in-law for decorating the church, and another sister-in-law for making my lovely white lace gown, and then I thanked my maid of honor for showing me what kind of man my groom was. Then Marcy and I paraded out of the sanctuary and I came home with her. You know the rest."

Another grin twitched the corners of his mouth and he laid down his napkin and his broad chest quivered slightly. "You actually stood there and thanked that two-bit hussy for helping break your heart?" he asked incredulously.

"Sure, she showed me his true colors. To top it all off she's my cousin . . . but she better keep her sorry hide away from any family reunions or I may still have to settle it with my fists, and Momma says that's not very ladylike," Lily said.

"Good grief, with relatives like that you don't need enemies. Didn't you cry?"

"Sure, later. On the way to Reagan I cried buckets and Marcy handed me a whole box of tissues. I think I used them all at least once and started over again before we got to the trailer. My eyes swelled shut, my nose ran, and I sniffled until Marcy threatened to pull over and throw me out on the side of the highway," she said. "Then I realized he wasn't worth any of it. He was a two-timing devil who didn't have the backbone to break it off even though he was leaving my house and going straight to her arms at night. But I still remember things he said and the way he looked in those white shorts and his clear blue eyes even when I don't want to," she said.

"That was a dirty trick." He nodded. "You should have put a twenty-two bullet between his eyes. Want more fish?" he changed the subject again, hoping to erase that haunted look from her eyes.

"I have already eaten so much it's sinful," she said.

It was close to midnight when the movie was over. Tears were streaming down her cheeks. She used a handful of napkins he'd picked up with the box of popcorn during intermission, and like she said about the tissues in the car, she used every one of them at least twice.

"Crying, still?" he asked when he opened the truck door for her.

"Maybe for a whole week," she snubbed. "I'm glad it's Friday and I don't have to go to school tomorrow. I may just sit on the couch and sob for two days." She blew her nose again.

"Want to see it again tomorrow night?"

"You're wicked." She slapped his arm.

"You really won't cry all weekend will you? You didn't even cry that long for old what's-his-name," Jesse said.

"He wasn't worth a whole weekend. He just broke my heart. That movie opened up my soul and a whole dam let go," she said. "Is that ice cream place open? I want a banana split."

"You serious?" he asked.

"I'm serious. Then I've still got the promise of a grand tour of your house. And then Mr. Elvis and I may watch the sun come up from your porch swing." She cocked her head to the side and made his mouth dry with desire.

But he shouldn't feel that way about Lily. Not after she'd called him *brother* Jesse just tonight.

Chapter Ten

Jesse led the way up onto the wide porch with a split cedar rail all the way around it. Two big rockers with a small table between them were on the north side, and a swing, just like the one on the back porch was on the other end. He held the door open for Lily and she stepped inside on the section of natural stone. He turned a dimmer switch beside the door and the lights in the living room slowly went from a twilight to a full-blown sunshine effect.

"So this is what it looks like when someone comes in the front door instead of the back." She was pleased that her voice came out normal. It sure didn't feel natural with Jesse standing beside her in those tight-fitting jeans.

"Yep," he nodded. "I can sit on the back porch in the early morning and watch the sun rise up over those trees like a big orange ball of fire. I can sit on the front porch with a cup of coffee in my hands at the close of a day and watch that same sun fall below the horizon. I've got the best of both worlds right here. See these stones? I gathered them out of the fields on my own property." He tapped the fireplace affectionately. "And this mantle. An old maple tree used to stand in our backyard at the home place. We had two swings in it when Marcy and I were little kids. One was an old tire on one rope and the other one was a real wood swing. The maple tree died about five years ago. I chose the longest length of the trunk and cured it out. This mantle is made from that chunk of black maple. These two picture frames"—he pointed to a couple of pictures of him and Marcy on the mantle—"I made them out of the rest of the wood."

"It's beautiful," she said in awe and appreciation. Not with as much astonishment for what he had built, but for the sentimental value he placed on them.

"The kitchen is like one in a magazine. Cabinets were custom designed to fit with a maximum of storage and a minimum of walking. I didn't want a formal dining room so this is what they call a . . ."

". . . country kitchen," she finished for him. "My mother likes a kitchen like this, too. She has a big table like that. We played games around it, did homework, fought, argued, and told stories. It was the center of our life."

"That's what I want." He smiled down at her. He stuffed his thumbs into his pockets to keep from putting his arm around her and drawing her close to him for a hug. "And on down the hall. Follow me for the rest of the tour, Miss Lily," he said in that slow Okie drawl that made her catch her breath. If only he wasn't a farmer . . . if only he didn't see a little sister when he looked at her . . . if only her silly heart wasn't on the rebound.

"As we pass the door on your left, please note there is a bathroom. Suitable for ladies with its big mirror and double sinks." He held up an imaginary microphone and talked into it like a bus tour guide. "Notice also there is running water and plumbing so the ladies don't have to get their feet wet in the morning dew chasing to the out house. And now on to the next door which is a huge linen closet with shelving to hold sheets and towels. Down the hall, please, watch your step now, the hardwood floors are very slick. Four bedrooms, two on each side. The master bedroom, if you will notice has a fireplace made of the same natural stone as the one in the living room. The bed is the four-poster out of my grandparents' house. It's the bed they took up housekeeping with and the one my dad was born in." He stopped abruptly.

She touched the wood, feeling the character and softness in the maple. "It's beautiful." She wished she could blank away the idea of other women visiting in this room, but she'd be living in a fool's paradise to think she was the first female who ever had the grand tour of his house, and what did it matter anyway. Lily Winslow was his *sister*. When he found the right woman, it wouldn't be someone with unruly curly hair and an attitude to go with it.

"I'm glad you like it," he said hoarsely. "Now would you like a Coke or a Dr. Pepper while you and Elvis watch the sun come up from my porch swing?"

"Yes, I would." She felt a strong need to get out of this bedroom and its drawing power. Mercy. She sure didn't need to let her emotions run rampant and land her in a bigger fire than she'd just escaped. Oh, but the pull was strong to snuggle down into Jesse's chest and feel his strong arms around her—but that would be incest since she was just his sister for the summer. As she followed him down the hallway back to the kitchen, she shut her eyes and tried to will up a picture of Dylan so she could get red-hot mad and chase away the bewildering thoughts in her mind. Or to visualize Jesse with another woman so she could turn pea green with jealousy, but neither one would materialize. All she could see was those bright green flecks in Jesse's light brown eyes and the way he smiled when he told her the story of the maple tree and the swings.

"Don't have any Coke or Dr. Pepper after all. I'll have to buy some next time I get to the store." He opened the refrigerator. "Got tea, though."

"I'll get the ice," she offered. Her hand brushed his and static electricity bounced around the room until she could almost hear the crackle. She willed her crazy, stupid heart to stop such nonsense right then. There wasn't room in her world or his for anything but friendship.

"Sit with me on the swing." He patted the side and started it swinging with his foot. "We sure need rain. But then we always need it in the dead middle of summer. If we see a drop fall out of the sky before August it'll be a miracle."

"Maybe you ought to call in the rain dancers," she said in all seriousness.

"Who?"

"The rain dancers. They're a bunch of gypsies. They come into town in a painted wagon pulled by six white horses. They don't work for free and the townspeople who want the rain have to take up a collection before they call the rain dancers. The poppa gypsy is the one who lights the fire and starts the smoke. The boy gypsies keep the fire fed with sticks. The momma gypsy and all the teenager rain dancers put on their bracelets and ankle janglers and dance around the fire. It's as graceful as a ballet the way they twirl the scarves and make a haunting, mystical music as all those bracelets jingle. Then pretty soon here comes a little bitty cloud and then it gets bigger and bigger and boom, the thunder rolls and it rains cats and dogs and baby elephants." She sipped her tea and bit her tongue.

"You've got to be kidding!" He'd bought the whole thing . . . lock, stock, and barrel full of lies.

"Yep, I am. You should see all those dead cats and dogs and baby elephants. When they hit the ground they splatter and guts go everywhere," she giggled and he slapped at her shoulder. Just the touch of her bare skin on his calloused palm made it sting with electricity. It was a wonder she couldn't see the flickering jolts dancing around them, but she seemed oblivious to anything but the joke she'd just pulled on him.

"You're awful. I thought you were being honest. Your eyes were as clear and bright as when you're telling me something really true. I'll have to watch you. You can lie like a pro," he grinned.

She chuckled. "Gotcha!"

His heart floated to the twinkling stars. This was the good life . . . swinging in the moonlight with a hot Oklahoma wind stirring the trees, icy cold tea in his hand, old Elvis sleeping on the rocking chair on the other side of the porch, and a good woman with a sense of humor beside him.

She set the glass on the porch railing and leaned back to watch the stars as he kept up a steady rhythm with his foot. They sparkled like diamonds in the jet-black sky. She remembered the solitaire on a wide band Dylan had given her and how it sparkled, but it couldn't compare with the stars. What he offered was just a fake brilliance compared with what she saw from Jesse's back porch. Next time she thought about a lifetime commitment, she was having a plain gold band and a trip to the judge's quarters in a courthouse somewhere. She might wear her jeans and boots or she might wear a dress, but she sure wasn't having a rehearsal dinner, a decorated church, a five-tiered cake or an expensive white lace dress. She would never repeat Lily's white lace wedding again. And she was having it all with a man just like Jesse Freeman . . . only with blond hair and who liked white shorts and polo shirts and who didn't know the first thing about a John Deere tractor or when to plant alfalfa.

Her eyes grew heavy with the constant motion. One minute she was listening to the crickets and frogs singing a forlorn melody and the next she was dreaming of a big ship. She wore a white lacy shawl and Dylan stood on the deck beside her with his arm around her shoulders and the warmth of his breath on her neck. He wore white slacks and a white knit shirt with a navy-blue collar and three buttons at the neck. An ocean breeze caused her to shiver and she leaned on his shoulder, snuggling down, enjoying the sensations of his powerful aftershave. Then a strange woman walked by and he kissed Lily on the cheek and was gone with nothing but an evil wink as he chased after the lady in the purple satin dress.

A sense of complete bewilderment filled her and in a fit of anger she threw the shawl over the guard rail of the ship. A man sighed in the shadows and called her name.

"Lily, why do you love him?" he asked softly.

Even though Dylan was gone, she could still smell the aftershave, and suddenly it wasn't Dylan's scent at all, but a strange one. And it came from the man just out of her reach in the shadows. Just a phantom with no face and a question she couldn't answer.

She snored loudly and a soft chuckle awoke her. She was snuggled down in Jesse's shoulder and he steadied her with an arm around her shoulders. It was his shaving lotion she was inhaling as she slept. The movie they watched earlier had put ships in her mind and the easy motion of the swing made her think of a boat ride. So it was all easy to understand. But that man in the shadows was her soul mate. It was written in indelible ink on her heart and she wanted to go back to sleep.

"You snored," Jesse laughed.

"Have for years. Thanks for not letting me sleep with my head thrown back. I'd have been in a world of hurt by morning. My poor old neck might have never been right again." She didn't move out of his embrace. "How much longer 'til the sun comes up?"

"An hour or so. You'll sleep all day tomorrow if you stay up and watch it." He didn't move his arm or readjust his position on the swing, either. "Thank goodness we don't have to plow or haul hay. I may sleep until noon and then laze around the house all afternoon, myself. I've got a whole sheaf of papers I need to grade before Monday."

"Watch the sun come up over the trees with me, and I'll help you do them when I wake up," she mumbled and went back to sleep.

Elvis curled up in her lap and purred loud enough to wake the dead but she just wrapped an arm around him in her sleep. If that's all he was going to talk out of the nice lady, he decided to be content with the meager offering and sleep with her.

Jesse's mind traveled in circles. Nothing had ever produced the contentment he felt while sitting in the swing that evening with his arm around Lily and listening to her occasional snores and Elvis' purrs.

His parents would be home tomorrow, in the middle of the morning or early afternoon, and things would be different then. He'd eat more meals there and then the harvest season would start and they'd be so deep into the hay, he'd have to make time for grading papers. Time to go out to The Fish Place and to movies that made her cry would be practically non-existent for the rest of the summer. Then she'd be gone. His heart did a nose dive and threatened to land on the porch at his boot tips.

"Hey, Lily," he wiggled her shoulder. "Better wake up and get your eyes open or you'll miss the show." He pointed to a faint orange glow just beginning to show through the green trees.

"Where, where, why didn't you wake me?" When she awoke it wasn't a slow, stretching movement, but a full-fledged eye-opener. "Oh, it's just beginning. Isn't it beautiful. Like a painter laid down a whole background of shades of orange, then painted the trees in front of it. Oh, look, Jesse, here it comes . . . like a pop-up pastry from the toaster. I'm hungry." Her eyes were almost as bright as the ball of fire coming up in the east.

"From painter to toasters to starvation," he smiled. "Your mind certainly runs in a strange groove."

"Wake up, Elvis." She shook the cat by a front paw. "You're going to miss the most beautiful sight in the whole world."

Elvis opened one eye. The female human had a very nice lap, but she wasn't very smart. Jesse never grabbed one of his paws and shook him just because it was getting light outside.

"I don't think he's interested," Jesse said. "Want a cup of coffee to go with the sunrise?"

"Oh, no, if you went in the house, you'd miss it, Jesse." She stood up and did a couple of bend-overs to stretch her muscles. "I've seen lots and lots of sunrises from the seat of a tractor and even some from the back of a hay-hauling operation we'd worked on all night, but none as pretty as that." She continued to watch the sky brighten as the new day was born.

"It is a bright ball of orange today," he nodded. He felt the emptiness in the swing. "Sure you don't want coffee? You said you were hungry."

"Nope, I'm fixing you a real breakfast to say thank you for the most wonderful night I've spent in ages and eons," she said. "Come on. Walk me home and I'll have an omelet and biscuits ready in half an hour." She tugged on his arm.

"You don't have to beg me," he laughed. "Elvis, old boy, you hold down the fort. I'll be back in a little while."

His hand brushed hers as they walked together down the path through the woods to the trailer. He carefully pulled it back, aware of the tingle, but she'd called him brother Jesse. Brothers did not touch their sister in the way he wanted to right then.

"Beat you to the trailer." She took off in a jog when they reached the clearing.

"What's the stakes?" he teased. "I ought to have a ten-yard head run since you slept two hours and I kept the cradle rocking."

"Nope, your legs are longer than mine so that evens the odds." She shook her head. "Stakes are lunch on Monday. At that restaurant out west of town."

"You're on," he said and sprinted ahead of her by three feet.

She gathered up the skirt of her dress and took off after him. Her foot hit the first step on the back porch about six inches before his did, and she turned around quickly to tell him he was a loser. Both of them felt the strings pulling them together like they were puppets controlled by someone much higher than they were. He hesitated and she paused and the moment was gone before either took advantage of the fleeting desire.

"I won," she grinned.

"I know," he laughed. "But I let you win. I knew you'd burn the omelet if I didn't let you win," he teased.

"You, kind sir, are full of bull, and you better bring lots of money on Monday because I'm sure I will have a healthy appetite after two classes of aerobics." She was scarcely even out of breath.

Jesse didn't mean to fall asleep on her couch. He was watching the morning news when she piled the breakfast dishes in the sink and declared she was having a shower and a long, long nap. She told him to lock the door when he left and she would see him later that afternoon to help him grade papers.

He awoke with a start when someone pounded on the front door of the trailer. He opened it to find his parents. They were both grinning like Cheshire cats. "So, y'all made it home?" A red blush crawled up his neck as he stepped back to let them inside and gave them both a hug.

"Yes, we did, is Lily still living here or did she go home?" his mother asked.

"She's still here," he said just about the time she came down the hall in a long nightshirt. She covered a big yawn with one hand and scratched her tangled hair with the other. "Jesse, is it already afternoon? Seems like I just fell asleep, and why did you knock! You never knock! Oh, hi, so y'all got home. We expected you today." She looked at the three strange people who were starting at her like she was naked. She looked down—yep, she had on clothes.

Jesse almost groaned. There wasn't even a pillow or a blanket on the sofa to back him up if he did try to make an excuse about falling asleep watching television. Gina Freeman wanted to laugh but she didn't want to offend either one of them. Warren Freeman had the feeling he'd just missed the punchline of a joke.

"Just thought we'd drop by and tell you supper is at our house tonight," Gina said. "Come on Warren. We've got to get to the grocery store and lay in supplies. The refrigerator is empty. Supper at six. You, too, Lily. Dominoes afterwards on the back porch. Bet we can whip these two old boys. See you then." She shoved her husband out the front door and left Jesse and Lily standing in the living room.

Bewilderment was written all over them.

"Good grief." He set his jaw firmly.

"What?" She looked around sleepily, then she started to giggle. "Good grief, Jesse, do you know what this looks like? You're barefoot, your jeans are all wrinkled and your shirt is pitiful, and you've been asleep. And here I came down the hall—" She got the hiccups and laughed until big tears rolled down her high cheekbones. She held her sides and fell back on the couch.

"Oh, hush, it's not that funny." He rolled his eyes. "Dad is going to tease me awful and Momma is going to start seeing some kind of white satin and roses." He sat down with a plop beside her. It was a messy situation and if he tried to talk himself out of it, he'd just end up making it sound worse than it was.

"But we weren't doing anything," Lily patted his knee. "It just looks like we did. Good grief, we're hardly even friends. I'm your *sister* and you're just good old *brother* Jess."

"Tell that to my folks," he groaned.

"I won't have to tell them anything," she said. "Your Dad has probably gone to get the shotgun to make me go to the church with you this afternoon and make an honest man out of you. I've taken advantage of you and ruined your reputation so now I guess I'll have to marry you. But if there's going to be white lace and flowers, honey, you have to wear them, because I refuse to ever do that again."

Chapter Eleven

"Okay," Gina said after supper. "Lily and I'll get the dishwasher loaded and you two get the dominoes out and wipe off the table on the back porch. We're going to teach you two a lesson you won't soon forget." It had been more than a week since they had returned from their trip to Mexico and she'd talked Lily and Jesse into eating with them every night. She'd reminded them that they had teaching in the mornings and most afternoons they farmed until dark, so it was easier for them to have supper with her and Warren.

"Yeah, 'bout like you whipped us last time," Jesse tormented but his eyes were on Lily rather than his mother.

"We let you win then so you wouldn't pout for days," Lily teased. "Tonight is payback."

"Wanna bet?" Jesse smarted right back.

"What's the stakes? Pecan pies for supper tomorrow night," Warren's green eyes twinkled.

"There won't be supper at home tomorrow night. You two are playing golf. We've got club tomorrow night at Janet Johnston's. It's our annual mother–daughter salad supper. Lily will have to stand in for Marcy. We'll leave at five and it's informally dress up. That means . . ."

"That means everyone wears something gorgeous and yet not satin and diamonds," Lily smiled. "I'd love to go with you. I can make potato salad. Mother is in a club and they have something like this every year."

Jesse moaned. "You mean we've got to eat microwave food at the clubhouse?"

"No, my whiny child. You and your father can go to any restaurant and eat whatever you want." She patted him on the head like a wayward child. "Now get out from under our feet."

Gina shut the back door and kept an eye out the window as she and Lily loaded the dishwasher.

"Ready?" Gina put the last spoon in the dishwasher. "Time to go teach them some manners. Warren thinks he's the best domino player in Johnston County."

"Well, I'm the best in Kansas," Lily laughed. "So let's draw up the lines, spit on our knuckles and dare them to cross it," she said. "But first, I do want to clear something up, Mrs. Freeman . . ."

"Gina. Just call me Gina. I got married when I was barely eighteen and I'm sure not old enough to be called Mrs. Freeman just yet," she laughed. "When I reach fifty next year, you can call me Mrs. Freeman, if you're not calling me mother by then."

"That's what I think I'd better clear up," Lily said. "What you saw in the trailer the other day wasn't what it looked like. Jesse and I went to The Fish Place that night then went to the movies. I wanted to watch the sun come up from his back porch. So we sat on the porch swing and then I fixed breakfast and went to bed. He was watching television and I suppose he went to sleep. Really, honestly, we're just . . . it's hard to explain. I'm not even sure we're friends. We're more like a brother and sister. We like the same things and I feel like a kid when we're together, but there's nothing romantic . . . really. He's been there when I needed him. But he's even said several times that I'm just family, another sister in his eyes, and I'm sure not ready for any type of relationship after what I just went through. Mostly what we do best is fuss and fight."

"Okay," Gina said. "I'll buy all of it because it has the ring of truth to it. But I know my son. Maybe even better than he knows himself, and we'll just see what the future has for us. For now, we better get us a box of tissues so they'll have something to wipe their tears on when we whip them soundly." She opened the back door.

Jesse looked up quickly, past his mother to the dark-haired beauty behind her. His mother noticed the sparkle in his eyes and the spontaneity he'd never had with any other woman. She was right. Jesse and Lily might not know it, and they sure wouldn't admit it, but love was on its way. Their hearts were already doing the courting dance. When that started, it didn't usually take long until the rest of the body followed.

Gina winked at Warren. He didn't have a problem with the arrangement. He liked Lily. She knew the ignition of a tractor from the back end of boar hog, and she was sure easy on the eyes. Someday he might set a little blue-eyed grandson on the tractor with him and buy him a red wagon to tote the puppies and kittens around the farm.

"Evenin'," Jesse said from the sofa late the next evening when she shoved the door to the trailer open. "How'd the dinner go? Did all those old hens cackle around you and tell you how beautiful you were?"

"Dinner was fine," she snipped and went back down the hall to change her clothes and attempt to get the sour taste out of her mind. She threw her dress on the bed and pulled on a pair of cut-off jean shorts and a chambray shirt.

"Somebody bad-mouth your potato salad? I thought the leftover bowlful you left in the fridge was pretty good." He smiled when she padded barefoot back into the living room.

"I met Amber," Lily said.

"Oh?"

"What is that supposed to mean?"

"Nothing," he said innocently.

"When she found out I was staying in Marcy's trailer she raised her eyebrows up to the sky and whispered that she knew where everything was in this trailer when you lived here."

Jesse blushed from the top of his dark hair all the way to the end of his toenails. "Well, at least you won't ask me again about whether I like women or not." He held up his arm and let it go limp.

"I'd like to mop up the streets of Tishomingo with all that long, blond hair," Lily snorted and Jesse cocked his head to one side. That didn't sound a bit like Lily. Sisters laughed at their brother's escapades and sometimes even chided them about being careful with loose women, but they never acted like they were jealous.

"Oh, and why would you do that?" he asked.

"She must judge all women by her own low-class self," Lily rolled her eyes. "She asked me if I was enjoying living with you out here in the boondocks. She made it sound like I'm some kind of hussy who's jumping your bones every chance I get," she declared vehemently and threw herself down on the far end of the sofa away from him. She tucked her chin down to her chest and looked up at him through mere slits where her big, blue eyes were just minutes before.

"Amber is the resident county bad girl." He cleared his throat and flipped through the channels on the television.

"Did you have a fling with her in this trailer?" Lily asked bluntly.

"Do you want to talk about your past? Show me yours and I'll show you mine," Jesse said.

"That's none of your business," she declared.

"I rest my case. Amber is mostly just brass," he nodded.

"She's mostly just dirty-minded hussy," Lily huffed.

"Are you going to jump my bones?" Jesse grinned.

"Sure, when the next blizzard hits Oklahoma in the middle of August, and when St. Peter and Lucifer join partnership to set up a snowcone stand at the front gates of Hades."

"I think I'll go home on that one," he chuckled as he made his way to the back door. He'd just figured out why Amber had come on to him so strong and so suddenly. It was because she heard Lily was living in

Marcy's trailer and she thought he and Lily were having an affair. Make something completely unattainable and it was suddenly passionately desirable. Just like the situation with him and Lily. It was purely fact that she wasn't interested in starting another relationship and especially not with farmer Jesse, so what does his crazy old heart do? It wanted just that.

"Oh, don't forget we've got a family reunion tomorrow," he said as he opened the back door.

"Oh," she moaned. "I've got to make a cake. I promised your mother I'd do a chocolate sheet cake."

"Do it in the morning," he suggested. "Isn't that one of those things you made for me one night when I was starving for chocolate? And you had it ready to eat in thirty minutes?"

"Good idea," she said. "Goodnight, Jesse."

"Night," he muttered as he closed the back door behind him.

She sat there on the sofa replaying the club meeting. It had been exactly the same as the ones she attended with her own mother in Kansas. Lots of women talking about the latest thing in town. Lots of good fattening food and exchanging of recipes. People were the same no matter where a woman hung her hat.

All but that hateful Amber. Had she cuddled up in his arms while they watched Mel Gibson movies on television? The fury inside of Lily turned into jealousy and confusion when she reminded herself that she had no right to any kind of feeling about Jesse's past loves.

She locked the doors and went down the hall to the bathroom where she stripped out of her clothes for the second time that evening and kicked them in the corner beside the hamper. She turned on the shower and stepped inside, hoping to wash away the ugly, black mood from her heart.

In the past month she'd run the entire gamut of passion. She felt like she'd been on an emotional roller coaster. First the numbness of finding out what a rascal Dylan was, then the anger and pain. A new friendship with Jesse. Jealousy. Frustration. She didn't want to be his sister.

But what did she want?

The hot water beat down with vengeance on the tight muscles in her neck and back as she tried to sort out her own feelings. She couldn't very well change his mind about her being his sister if she didn't even know what she wanted. He'd never once led her to believe that he would be interested in anything other than a platonic relationship.

Finally she shut the water off and wrapped herself up in a big towel. She checked in the mirror. Same woman. Same blue eyes with a spark of anger and jealousy. Same hair. But Jesse had brought out something other than brassy sass in her and she couldn't put her finger on what it was.

It didn't matter anyway. She didn't even need to sort it out because no matter what her silly heart said, Lily was not getting involved with a farmer. And that could truly be written in stone and set down for all future generations.

Chapter Twelve

Lily picked up two baskets with covered dishes inside. It was the nine millionth Freeman family reunion, held the Saturday after July Fourth every year since right after Adam and Eve got evicted from the Garden of Eden. The Freemans figured the garden was actually in Reagan, Oklahoma, so they'd all converged upon this little picnic area for so long no one could remember the first time. But they tried every year and that was the main topic of discussion if no one had a new baby, a new wife, a new girlfriend, or a new divorce to mull over.

At least that's the story Jesse told her when the Freemans had insisted she join them for the reunion. He picked up a cooler with a smoked ham nestled down inside and led the way to the tables already loaded with enough food to feed all of Johnston County.

"Hey, Jesse," an old fellow called out and gave him a thumbs-up sign and a big, toothless grin.

"Guess we won't need to worry about when the first reunion was this year," Jesse told Lily. "I think you're the new topic this year. Do me a favor. Pretend you're really with me . . . I mean, like a real date thing . . . it'll make their day."

"It'll cost you," she smiled up at him. "I only do acting and pretending for a price. And it's pretty steep," she whispered seductively so everyone would think she was whispering sweet love words in his ear.

"By the hour, or by the job?" he leaned down like he was going to kiss her.

"Whoa. Kisses cost extra. Cheeks are one price, foreheads another and then lips. I don't know if you got enough to pay that kind of bill," she informed him. "You might have to sell the farm and hock old Elvis."

"Whew, you drive a hard bargain." The green flecks in his eyes danced and the dimple in his cheek deepened. Her insane heart skipped around like real gypsies doing a rain dance when Jesse pretended to kiss her, and in a moment of abandonment, she wished she had the courage to wrap her arms around him—right there in front of God and every Freeman that could be lassoed and hauled to the reunion—and really kiss him.

"Yep, I do." She combed her hair back with her fingertips and wrapped a rubber band around a ponytail of auburn curls. "So am I your sister, Lily, for free—or your woman for pay?" she continued to torment him.

"Got a price in mind, so I know how much to mortgage my place for?"

"Oh, I'm expensive. You have to take me to dinner every Friday night for the rest of the summer. That's only two times before I go back to Kansas. But it's my choosing and no comments about how much I eat," she said.

"Maybe you better be my free sister. Don't know if the farm is worth that much," he flirted blatantly as he slipped an arm around her shoulders and steered her toward the older family members sitting in a semicircle of lawn chairs. When his fingertips touched the softness of her bare shoulder, a jolt of pure desire shot through his body.

"Uncle Joe, meet Lily Winslow," he introduced her to the man in the first chair. "This is Aunt Molly," he nodded toward the chubby lady sitting next to the tall, lanky man.

"Pleased to make your acquaintance." Uncle Joe stuck out his bony hand to shake with her. "You 'bout the prettiest thing Jesse ever brought around. Sight for these old sore eyes."

"Oh, hush," Aunt Molly said. "You'll be runnin' her off." The short, little woman stood up and hugged Lily. "Jesse's a fine man," she whispered slyly.

Lily nodded and winked.

"You kids get on over there. They've got a badminton game over by the old church and a croquet game gettin' set up over there," she pointed to the left. "And before long they'll have the music starting up. You sing any, Miss Lily?"

"Little bit," Lily said.

"Then Jesse will have to give you up for a little

while. We don't care if you sing country or gospel. Just not any of that rock stuff. That sounds like a truckload of hogs run into a truckload of china dishes. Ain't fittin' to listen to. So don't get out there playing games and get to screamin' and hollerin' and ruin your voice. We'll expect to hear from you after dinner," Molly said.

So the Freeman family, or at least one named Molly figured Jesse was a fine man. *How do I feel?* she asked herself. *I sure got my dander up last night at the club dinner. Do I feel something other than brotherly love for Jesse? It would be fighting a losing battle because he made it pretty clear he's not interested in me except for a little play acting. I'm just an adopted part of the family for a day.*

"Name your game," Jesse hugged her even closer. "Croquet, badminton, Frisbees. Looks like they're setting up dominoes under that shade tree over there."

"Well, let's see," she snuggled up closer to his side, "if I was really your sweetheart today, then we would probably want to be alone, not in the middle of a big game of croquet. So we should hold hands and stroll across the street to the store, buy a soda pop and take a walk down that dirt road. That way they'd all have a free half-hour to decide whether I'm going to be accepted or blackballed."

"Sounds like you've played at being a paid woman before." He grabbed her hand and headed for the store. Every time he touched her his skin tingled. Strange that the woman of his dreams, a tall blond like Amber, had never had that effect on him. Yet, here was Lily, short, dark-haired, and impish who made his blood boil. And she thought he was her brother. There was no justice in the world.

"We'll get a canned pop from the machine, in plain view of everyone. They're all a betting bunch. I've seen them bet nickels on which fly will fly away from a watermelon rind first. So they'll make bets on whether you drink RC or Coke, so decide now," he said.

She didn't care which machine they put money in, she just hoped he could do it with one hand and not let go of her hand with the other one. She swept her long, gauzy broomstick skirt away from the posts around the single gas pump, and stopped long enough to bend over to smell the flowers in the old footed bathtub beside the wooden porch of the only store in Reagan. A place to purchase gas, a gallon of milk, or a loaf of bread. The whole store should have been the front cover of a Louis L'Amour western book, not sitting in the middle of Oklahoma in the first year of the twenty-first century. The bright red soft drink machine looked out of place just a few feet away from an old wringer-type washing machine and a couple of weather-beaten church pews.

It was the last of an era hanging on while the new one was trying desperately to be born. *Kind of like your heart,* her mind said. *You're letting a heartache hang on while your heart is trying desperately to shake it off. It's time to give birth to a new relationship, Lily. Maybe not with this man holding onto your hand and making your heart flutter with excitement today but with someone who's interested in the things you are. This old store building will crumble one of these days . . . let the bad experience with Dylan crumble and sweep it out the back door of your heart.*

In the time it took to cross the street Lily came to terms with herself. She was ready to think about a future that didn't have Dylan Reeder even if a future with Jesse Freeman wasn't an option. But they could be friends. They could even pretend to be more for today. Just for fun. And she'd remember him fondly when she went home to Kansas in a couple of weeks.

"Coke?" Jesse fished in the pocket of his jeans for change, but he held tightly to her hand.

"RC," she said, glancing over her shoulder. Jesse was right. The knights of the round circle of lawn chairs were watching them without blinking. When he handed her a cold red, white, and blue can of RC, she saw Molly playfully slap Joe and hold out her hand. He fished around in the bib pocket of his overalls and put a bill of some kind in her hand. She shoved it down the front of her dress somewhere in that big bosom and Lily was glad she made the right choice.

"So what does a paid woman do when she walks down the dirt road with her fellow?" Jesse whispered like he was afraid his voice would carry back to the picnic area.

"She drinks her cold soda pop slowly and then they turn around and walk back, letting everyone watch them," she told him. *At least that's the way they do things in the books I read before you rescued me out of the deep pity pool I was about to drown in,* she thought. Her hand fit into his perfectly and she noticed his palm was just about as clammy as her own. Probably from carrying the ham to the picnic tables. There was no way she affected him the same way he did her.

He'd stated his position on that issue the day after he found her sprawled out in the woods behind his house.

Just before they would have disappeared over a small hill she stopped. "It's time to go back now. Don't let go of my hand and walk slowly."

"Why here?" he asked.

"Because they will lose sight of us," she giggled. "We have to put on a good show. You're paying dearly for it. I'm thinking maybe that new steak house would be a good start next Friday night." She gazed up into his face like a lovesick actress on daytime television. Suddenly, she didn't know if she was play acting in this game . . . or if it was all real.

Jesse moaned. But he was having so much fun he would have paid more than just dinner. *Two weeks she'll be gone back to Kansas. And I'll be back paddling the same boat Blake does. Oh, no, I won't,* he made up his mind firmly. *I may be a lifelong bachelor and the oldest one sitting over there in a few years. But when I am as old as Uncle Joe, I'll look down the road, and I'll remember a pretty dark-haired woman in my memories. One who made me laugh one day when I was a young man. One who was my friend for a little while, and pretended to be more for a day. Maybe I'm ready to settle down now and start a family. All this pretend must be getting to me.*

"Pretty quiet, all of a sudden." She swung her hand in his as they walked.

"Just thinking," he said seriously enough to make little chills on her arms in spite of the blistering heat.

"About what?" she asked, then wished she could take back the words.

"About how much I'm enjoying this game," he said.

"Here, let me set you up on the porch. Good effect you know." He put his arms around her waist and lifted her up on the porch, then hopped up beside her. She threw her empty can in a battered old trash barrel beside the ice machine under a swinging sign advertising minnows and worms. He pulled her hand hard enough to spin her around. One minute she was thinking about what songs she would sing after lunch, the next she was plastered next to Jesse, hearing the fast beat of his heart, and his arms around her.

"I guess you better figure in a kiss on the lips," he whispered as he used his rough, callused hand to tilt back her chin. He tasted the sweet flavor of RC Cola and heard the tingle of bells somewhere in the distance. Surely there was a train or someone rang the church bells. This kind of thing only happened in those romance books his mother read, or on afternoon television. She shivered when his tongue teased her lower lip and she thought she heard fireworks somewhere in the distance. Probably a bunch of kids with a leftover supply from the Fourth of July.

"Whew, that kind of kiss will really run the bill up," she giggled nervously.

"Worth it." He led her back across the street. "Look at Joe. Betcha he and Molly could tell us a story about another day and time." He talked fast to cover up the way the kiss affected him.

"Welcome to the nine millionth Freeman family reunion." Jesse took his place behind the microphone set up under the shade trees after lunch. "These boys say I've made the welcome address so long now it's my official yearly job. We'll ask Uncle Joe to say our prayer, now." He took his straw hat off and bowed his head.

"Dear lord, we are grateful for this beautiful day and good family . . ." Uncle Joe said in a raspy old voice. Lily shut her eyes and a thousand memories invaded the dark space in her mind. There was Jesse rounding the corner of the trailer, demanding that she tell him who she was; Jesse giving her the thumbs-up sign when they had the plowing contest; Jesse with his elbows on the counter top watching her make a cobbler. Then like an icy wind, there was Dylan in his white tennis shorts and that fantastic tan, beckoning with his forefinger for her to join him. She snapped her eyes open just before Uncle Joe said, "Amen."

"Now, it's time for lounging in the shade and nibbling on leftovers all afternoon," Jesse said and one of the young men behind him handed him a guitar. "My special friend, Miss Lily Winslow is on the entertainment committee and will be singing for us. So if you'll join us, Lily." He held out his hand and she stepped up to the microphone.

"This going to cost me?" he whispered.

"Nope, singing is free today," she whispered back. "You boys know anything by Dolly?" she asked the band members behind her.

"You just name your poison and we'll do our best to keep up," one of them said.

She grabbed the mike and adjusted the stand. "Here goes. Put your little hands together and clap occasionally if you want me to keep on," she said to the Freeman family and took off on a fast tune. Aunt Molly gave her a thumbs-up sign and before long everyone was keeping time by clapping or tapping their feet.

"One last song to finish the show," she said an hour later. "At home, we always close with a hymn. This is for Aunt Molly who has stolen my heart away," she said as she began "Amazing Grace." By the time she finished the elderly lady was dabbing her old blue eyes with the tail of her white apron and Uncle Joe pulled out a big red bandanna from his hip pocket and blew his nose.

"I'm expecting that same song tomorrow morning in church," a middle-aged man said in the crowd when the last note died in the hot July summer wind.

"Yes, sir," she saluted.

"Didn't know you could sing like that!" Jesse took her hand led her to a wash tub full of soda pop chilling in crushed ice.

"I'm spittin' dust," she smiled. "I need something cold and wet. Didn't know you could play like that!" she countered.

"It's just a pass time thing," he said. "Boys over there play a lot, but I only pick it up now and then. But you could be in Nashville."

"Don't want what it all entails. Never did. I want a normal family, Jesse. Not ten months out of every year on the road and never seeing my husband or kids. So I just sing at church pretty often on Sunday and for the harvest party in the fall at home," she said as she reached for the cold can of Dr. Pepper he held out for her. She had to let go of his hand to pull the tab.

"You got to trust someone if you want a family," Jesse reminded her as he guzzled back half a can of Dr. Pepper.

"I may change my mind someday but it'll be a long time down the road," she said seriously.

Chapter Thirteen

Lily sat on the deck until midnight watching the moon rise higher and higher in the sky. There was a fairy ring and she almost trotted out across the woods to wake Jesse up so he could see it. Fairy rings didn't appear very often. She'd only seen two or three in her lifetime. It was a strange setup when the moon and one lonely old star did a dance in the middle of a bunch of clouds. The clouds became the fairies and if she squinted her eyes and stretched her imagination they really were enchanted imps cavorting around the moon and star.

There was the bonus of a wish in store. Besides the literal beauty of watching the fairy ring she could wish for anything she wanted. Would she wish that Dylan would come back to her and beg for forgiveness? They were so much in love and everyone said they were the most beautiful couple they'd ever seen. All men made mistakes. Even that witchy Amber had let her know that Jesse had sown some wild oats. But he wasn't engaged to another woman when he was sowing and Dylan had been.

No, she wouldn't wish for even a minute of a life with Dylan. She couldn't trust him and she wouldn't live with a man she couldn't trust. Not even if they were the cutest couple in the whole state of Kansas. She leaned her head back in the reclining lawn chair and shut her eyes tightly. She simply wished for the contentment she'd known all day long at the Freeman family reunion to stay with her forever. That someday she'd find a man like Jesse. A virtual knight-in-shining-armor. One to make her laugh and who would could stand proudly with her in front of family and friends. One who would not be married to his land.

When she opened her eyes the fairy ring was gone, the moon and star had long since shut up shop and gone away for the day, and a new morning was dawning. She moaned as she wiggled her head to get the kinks out of her neck. She checked her watch. She'd spent the whole night on the deck in the lawn chair. It was only a couple of hours until church time.

She tried a few stretching exercises to get her aching muscles back into shape. As she started into the trailer, she stepped on a slug and commenced to do something between a watusi and an old hippy breakdance. Finally she made herself calm down and walked on the back of her heel into the living room and down the hallway to the bathroom where she wadded toilet tissue around her hand and swiped at the slimy mess scrunched up between her toes.

Her nose snarled as she got most of the abominable dead creature off her foot and thought about how funny Jesse would think the whole thing was when she related the tale to him. She washed her foot until it was pink and she couldn't feel sticky goo between her toes when she scrunched them together.

So much for wishing for contentment, she thought as she took a fast shower. Evidently her wish had gotten tangled up in the pecan trees at the end of the deck. Because there was nothing calming or peaceful about waking up and stomping the life out of a slug.

"Lily, you ready?" Jesse called out as he opened the front door two hours later. "Momma and Dad are waiting in the truck."

"Just putting on my shoes," she yelled from the bedroom.

"Whoooo." He raised an eyebrow. "Don't you look like an angel this morning?"

"Most angels have long silky blond hair and they don't wear fire-engine red," she told him emphatically, rolling her light eyes toward the ceiling.

"Well, they should if they look like you." He held the door for her.

"You look pretty handsome yourself." She eyed the freshly starched jeans and crisply ironed white western shirt. A black bolo tie matched his black leather dress boots and black Stetson.

"Thank you ma'am. Best a poor old dirt farmer can do with limited means. He'll be in the poorhouse after he pays yesterday's bill," he teased. When they were in the back seat of the club cab truck, he slid across the seat until she could feel the starch in his shirt on her bare arm. He reached across her lap and picked up her hand, and it was her turn to raise an eyebrow.

"I'm not wiped out yet. Charge me up with another day," he whispered seductively in her ear, and she jerked her head up to see Gina watching them in the rear-view mirror.

They found a pew in the front of the church with a space left for four people. Announcements were made and then the preacher took his place behind the pulpit. Her heart fluttered. She'd sang since she was a little girl in church and at family reunions. But something about Jesse leading her into the church that morning with her hand firmly in his told her he sure wasn't feeling like her older brother and her crazy heart was liking the sensation way too much.

It had to be a rebound thing. She'd been hurt and now it was time for a relationship where she would wake up madly in love again. She liked the affection she had with Dylan and she would like to experience it again. But someone forgot to tell her idiot heart that Jesse Freeman was not the right man to play the rebound game with.

"We've got a wonderful surprise this morning," the preacher said. "Jesse has brought a guest today, and she's agreed to bring us some special music. I was privileged to hear her sing yesterday at the Freeman family reunion in Reagan. I'm afraid we don't have a band like they had yesterday, but I did find a couple of background tapes. I really don't think she needs them. She could probably sing with the angels in the pearly gates with no music behind her at all. But I can see I'm making her blush as red as the pretty dress she's wearing this morning, so I'll hush and let you be the judge. Miss Lily Winslow." He offered his hand from the pulpit.

She didn't have a choice but to stand up and go forward to sing. She glanced down at the note with her name at the top and saw three old gospel songs. Before the music started for the first one she took time to offer a silent, brief prayer of thanks that she had sung them many times in her own church.

In the middle of the first song, the doors at the back of the church swung wide open and there stood Amber, in a white lace suit and high-heeled shoes that made her look at least seven feet tall. She shut the doors with a loud bang, marched to the front of the church and sat down in the pew right beside Jesse who whispered something in her ear. She gave him a look that would have fried the tail off the devil himself. Then she jumped up like she'd been shot with a bolt of lightning and sat in the pew behind the Freeman family.

Lily didn't miss a note, but a vision of that woman parading right to the front of the church and dragging her out to the church parking lot for a fight did flit through her mind somewhere in the middle of "Precious Memories."

Chapter Fourteen

Lily tossed and turned. The pillow was too hard, the bed too soft. She kicked the covers off because it was too hot. Then the air conditioner clicked on and she tugged them back up because it was too cold. She made a mental list of last-minute things she needed to do. Tomorrow she was going home. For a couple of days at her folks' house to visit everyone and then back to her own apartment. The idea of her own bathroom, her own frayed towels and even her own cracked teapot excited her.

Jesse offered to drive her home even though either one of her brothers or even her good friend, Vivien Hollister, from the farm adjoining the Winslow place, would have gladly come to get her. But Jesse wanted to go with her and she was eager for her mother to meet her new friend she'd talked about all summer.

She'd barely gotten to sleep when the alarm clock started to buzz—6:00. Time to get up. She had a special surprise for Jesse this morning. She had made her special cinnamon rolls the night before and all she had to do was pop them in the oven for thirty minutes. Jesse Freeman was getting breakfast in bed that morning. She giggled and hoped he didn't sleep in the buff. That would embarrass both of them. Him more than her, she was sure.

She slipped into a pair of shorts and tee-shirt she'd left out of her suitcase when she packed the night before. She buckled her sandals and pulled her hair up into a ponytail. Excitement filled every fiber of her being. She was going to surprise Jesse with breakfast for all the care he'd given her through the previous six weeks. For the times when his stubbornness outweighed hers, when she didn't want him around and he came anyway. When he teased her into finding a life again, and getting her a job and so many, many more things he'd done to make her summer pass quickly.

The aroma of fresh baking cinnamon rolls filled the trailer. She fidgeted as she waited for the rolls to finish baking. Finally, they were just the right shade of brown and she dumped them upside down on the tray she had ready, then smothered them with a quarter pound of pure melted sweet butter. It was a pure love offering. Not love as in passionate love but love as in thank you. There was a vast difference.

She picked up the metal tray by the bamboo handles and gingerly made her way around the pond and to the edge of the woods. She heard the crunch of gravel as an automobile made its way down the lane. The Freemans must have been out early. Probably pulling a calf, since she'd heard Warren talking about a heifer about ready to give birth.

She kept a sharp eye out for those killer rabbits on the path through the narrow spanse of woods but they must have been sleeping in that morning. She crossed the backyard and set the tray on the edge of the porch while she fished a back door key from the fake rock in the flower bed. Right where she'd seen Jesse put it one night when they came home from eating at the steakhouse in Ardmore.

She eased the back door open, left her shoes, wet with dew, on the back porch and picked up her offering. She was all the way across the kitchen before she looked up and there stood Amber with her arms around Jesse's neck. She'd dropped her white silky robe in a muddle on the floor and one spaghetti strap of her nightgown was slipping off her shoulder. All Jesse wore was a pair of silky-looking black boxer shorts.

"Oh." The single word escaped Lily's mouth in something between an embarrassed moan and a sick sigh.

"What are you . . . ?" Amber turned abruptly.

"Lily? This is not what it looks like." Jesse frowned.

Lily calmly opened the pantry door and raked all the cinnamon rolls into the trash can, poured the coffee down the sink in the kitchen, set the thermos on the cabinet and stormed out the back door, slamming it so hard she heard the glass rattle as she picked her wet shoes up from the back steps and jogged barefooted—all the way to the trailer. She threw herself on the couch. Her face was scarlet and she wanted to hit something. Anything. It didn't matter what. Jesse

Freeman would do just fine if he'd just walk through that back door. Amber would do even better if she'd show up on the deck. She heard a car race down the lane and skid on the loose gravel out onto the paved road. She didn't care if it was Amber and Jesse on the way to the justice of the peace to say "I do," in their white lace and black silk boxers. She was going home today anyway, and it didn't matter what he did.

One thing for absolute sure. There was no way Jesse Freeman was driving her home. She'd walk the whole two hundred and fifty miles or else call her mother or Vivien to come get her. She stomped back to the bathroom and raked the rest of her toiletries into a tote bag. Makeup, toothpaste, hair spray, and a hand mirror all clattered together.

"She's probably been going over there every night and that's why he didn't need a woman," she muttered. "Well, what's it to me if he's tumbling the sheets with good old Amber? Not one thing. She can have him. I'm sure not interested." She snapped her makeup kit shut with a pop.

"Lily, where are you?" Jesse came down the hall like a bull elephant.

"Go away." She stepped out of the bathroom, her eyes barely slits and her mouth set in a firm line. "I'll walk to Kansas before I ride a mile with you."

"I'm taking you home today. I said I would and I will." His face was scarlet with rage. The veins on his neck were pulsating and his hands were doubled into fists that made his biceps strain the knit of his shirt sleeves.

"No, you are not. I'm callin' Momma and she'll either drive down or send someone if she's too busy with the harvest crew. I don't need this, Jesse. If you want to shack up with her on the sly . . ." She turned in the narrow hallway and screamed at him.

"I have not been sleeping with Amber." He raised his voice and stomped his foot hard enough to rattle the pictures on the walls. "I got up early this morning and didn't even have coffee made when someone knocked on the front door. I opened it and Amber walked in, dropped her robe, and put her arms around me just about the time you walked in the back door. I didn't invite her to my house, Lily." He crossed his arms over his chest and dared her to say a word.

"Oh, sure," she challenged. "And I'm the queen of the Nile. Just get out of here and leave me alone. I came down here to get my mind together. A peaceful little month of solitude. I didn't ask for all this."

"I'm telling the truth. It wasn't what it looked like. I sent her home and she won't be back again. Remember when Mom and Dad came home and you came out of the bedroom scratching your head and yawning. What did it look like then? Remember what they thought. Well, you thought wrong today," he threw back at her. "And I'm taking you home. You're just mad and . . ."

"You bet, I'm mad," she said. "I'll be so glad to get back to the city where I belong, I may do a stomp dance in the middle of Main Street under the traffic light. And I hope I never, ever see Amber or any other two-bit hussy like her again and if I never see Reagan or Tishomingo, Oklahoma again it'll be too soon."

Chapter Fifteen

They arrived at her folks' farm just a few minutes before lunch. She called her mother the night before to tell her what time they were leaving. She sure hadn't taken time to call her that morning before they left. Not after the fracas with Amber. All June Winslow knew was Jesse this and Jesse that for the past six weeks. Then suddenly Jesse were there and Lily acted like he had a bad case of leprosy. Something must have happened on the trip. June remembered her daughter plainly saying just last night, "Jesse says he's bringing me home since I don't have a vehicle down here. You'll like him, Momma. I didn't like him one bit at first but he grows on a person. He's really my friend."

"You want me to make up two beds or one?" her mother laughed.

"Momma!"

"Don't you Momma me. I was just teasing you.

Friend or lover, Jesse Freeman will sleep in his own bedroom, and you in yours. I'm anxious to meet him, though. Don't eat lunch on the way. The girls and I are cooking for the harvest crew anyway. Your brothers and the grandkids will be here," June Winslow said.

"Poor old Jesse will think the whole county is there," she moaned.

"They will be, and ninety percent of them are family," June said.

She had fought a legion of demons on the way to Coffeyville. She seethed in her own anger for hours, answering his questions with one-syllable words and daring him to bring up the subject of Amber crawling into his bed. She didn't care who Jesse slept with, not that it mattered anyway. Good grief, by the time he got her home and safely dumped on her parents' front porch he'd be lighting a shuck back to southern Oklahoma. She was just a friend and a poor one at that right now. One who believed the enemy's word against his; one who'd pouted all the way from southern Oklahoma to Kansas.

That wasn't even the biggest thing she worried about. Even though she looked forward to being home, there was no doubt somewhere along the way she would meet Dylan again. After all, Independence was just a few miles from Coffeyville. What would she do if her knees went weak when she saw Dylan again? What if Rachel was tired of him and he wanted to give their relationship one more chance? What if he was truly sorry for the mistake he made? It had been so easy to think about him being gone completely from her heart when she was in southern Oklahoma with every minute of every day taken up by school or Jesse, but it might be a different matter when she got back to her old friends and stomping grounds.

The closer they got to Coffeyville, the more agitated she became. They were met in the backyard by scores of people, brothers, sisters-in-law, field hands, children of all sizes and ages, and June and Mitch Winslow. June in a pair of worn jeans and a faded tee-shirt, her salt and pepper hair pulled up into a ponytail. Mitch, in bibbed overalls and a work-stained chambray shirt, his dark hair curling up around his old work cap.

"Got your beauty from your mother, and your hair from your dad," Jesse said when they got out of his truck. Then they were completely surrounded and separated by family. Talk around the dinnertable turned to wheat and hay. The hard red winter wheat had come in good in spite of the drought. The price wasn't as high as they'd hoped, but the per acre yield was good enough to make up for the slight drop in per bushel price.

"What can I do to help?" Jesse dipped into the mashed potatoes and gravy for seconds. "I can manage a combine, or I can drive a truck back and forth to the elevators if you point me in the right direction. I'd planned to stay until Sunday morning."

"Appreciate the offer," Mitch nodded. This was the kind of man he'd envisioned for Lily all of her life. One who could set up to a harvest table under the shade trees and enjoy his vittles, and who knew the difference in hard red winter wheat and soybeans.

"I can use a driver to take the wheat to the elevators this afternoon," Mitch said. Lily looked up and saw a mischievous look in his eyes. "But this evening is another matter. I expect Lily and her mother need to catch up on some visitin' while they get supper ready. But I don't know whenever we're going to get that hay out of the field and into the barn. Reckon you two could haul a little hay tonight?"

"Sure," Jesse nodded. "Lily can drive the bale loader and I'll pitch it," he volunteered her and she kicked him hard under the table.

"Ouch," he moaned. "Now why'd you do that, Lily?"

"Don't volunteer me without asking," she snapped.

"Yes, ma'am," he nodded. "Miss Lily, in view of the fact that I need a driver for a bale loader this evening, so I can help your dad, would you do me the honor of driving for me?" he asked in mock meekness.

"Thank you, *brother* Jess," she said sarcastically, drawing out the word "brother" like it was a dirty word. "I would love to drive a hay truck for you this evening." *And you better get ready to load hay like Superman,* she thought. *Because I'm still madder than a wet hen after a tornado. And besides you weren't invited to stay until Sunday. I was expecting you to unload my suitcases and get on back across the border. Amber is probably waiting with an apology and open arms in that sexy white gown. White lace. If I never see white lace again, it'll be too soon.*

The hay truck wasn't air conditioned but at least the scorching summer sun had long since set, and the night air, though hot wouldn't burn Lily to a red-lobster crisp. She adjusted the cushion in the driver's seat and hopped inside. The field reminded her of Easter. All those bales of alfalfa laying there, shining in the moonlight, like eggs waiting to be picked up in a field of grass. For a fleeting moment she wished she was a little girl again in a fancy frock when all that mattered was finding the prize egg at the Easter egg hunt. A time when hormones were dormant, and the opposite sex had no appeal.

"Ready?" she yelled to the back of the truck where Jesse waited.

"Ready," he said, and she watched as he cocked his work hat to the back of his head and got ready to stack the hay on the back of the flatbed truck.

Lily turned the key in the ignition and started the engine. She wiggled down into the pillow on the seat and stretched her leg out to reach the clutch, stomped it, and grabbed the floor shift. She edged up to the first bale and the machinery did its work, throwing the hay up on the conveyor belt and back at Jesse to stack neatly. It was alfalfa and a lot heavier than stubble hay, but Jesse handled it like he was dealing with marshmallows. She watched the muscles in his upper arms flex as he caught the bales and stacked them like a pro.

Dylan had muscles like that but it was from swinging a tennis racket and working out in the gym. He would have sooner signed his own death certificate than stacked hay all night for her father. Dylan's tan didn't stop in the middle of his big muscles like Jesse's did and when Dylan peeled off his shirt his back and neck were the same color. When Jesse took his shirt off and sprawled out in the living room floor at the trailer, his back was paler than his neck and arms. She'd sworn she wasn't going to spend the rest of her life with a man with a farmer's tan, and she fully well intended to stand by that vow.

She looked in the side mirror and could see Jesse sitting on top of the load as she backed into the barn to unload. By the time she cut the engine, crawled out of the truck, and grabbed a pair of hay hooks, he already had six bales thrown off the back and tossed over for her to sink the hooks into and stack in the barn.

"Slave driver," she said tartly. "We could have a five-minute break to catch our breath. Daddy won't fire you, you know? Not when you work for free."

"Never know." He gave her one of those half-grins and reminded her again of that picture in the cafe downtown. If he pulled a Kist soda pop from behind him and tilted the bottle back for a long drink, she'd swear he was just an apparition from another age and time. "Got to work hard and make a good impression," Jesse said, solidifying the fact he was indeed more than a ghost. "He might not give me a place to put my tired old head tonight, if I don't get this field cleaned off. Reckon he'll want it plowed under tomorrow?"

"Good grief, I hope not. You'll volunteer me to do it," she said.

By the time they unloaded the first truckful she was panting, and Jesse's blue work shirt was soaked. "Ready to go again?" she huffed. She wasn't about to admit she was ready to drop from physical as well as mental exhaustion.

"Til it's done," he said. "Two more trucks and we should have it finished. Betcha we can get it in and stacked by two in the morning, sneak in four hours of sleep and not even miss breakfast. Is it served up under the trees or in the house?" Jesse asked.

"You *are* a slave driver. Bet you got a whip stuck in your back pocket," she sighed as she crawled back into the cab of the truck.

Sometime well after midnight they finished the job. When they got back to the house, Jesse took a long shower and let the hot water work on the muscles in his back. He wished that he could go downstairs to Lily's room to beg for a massage. As angry as she was though, she might put a twenty-two slug between his shoulder blades rather than a puddle of alcohol. He toweled off and slipped between the cool, crisp white sheets, and expected to be asleep before his head even hit the pillow. But he was wide awake thinking about Lily. Why couldn't she believe him? Hadn't she ranted and raved about the girl when she'd gone to the club supper with his mother? And now she was in a snit over something that he had no control over. *Women.* He could make a nuclear power plant from a coat hanger and Silly Putty easier than understanding a woman.

He would never be able understand her—*even if he was in love with her.* The thought made him sit straight up in bed in a cold sweat just like he'd awakened from a terrible dream. In love with Lily . . . really, truly in love with her. Now that was a nightmare for real. She didn't want anything to do with farmers and she said she was going to do a stomp dance on the Main Street of town. It wouldn't do him a bit of good to fall in love with her.

He threw himself back on the pillows and thought about the day of the reunion: the way she stood up there and sang to the whole family, and the way she'd pretended to be his date. But mostly about the way his breath caught in his chest when he kissed her on the front porch of the old country store.

Jesse had barely fallen into the bed and shut his eyes when the bedroom door eased open. Lily had better not be sneaking into his room right here in her folks' house. If she was he didn't know whether to pretend to be asleep or hide under the bed until she ran out of bullets. She'd certainly hadn't given him one minute's worth of smiles or sweet talk last night. It was just work, work, and more work. Even when they got to the house she'd simply said goodnight and disappeared behind her bedroom door. He threw his forearm across his eyes and moaned.

"Wake up sleepyhead," Lily giggled as she bounced on the bed. She was fully dressed in faded jeans and a clean work shirt. A few curls had already escaped from her ponytail. "Daylight is almost here and Momma is making biscuits. Time to get up and face the morning." She pulled his arm away from his eyes, her touch sending another one of those shocks of desire through his body.

"Well, why didn't you say so." His eyes were wide open. "What made you so happy and cheery this morning?"

"I like mornings," she said simply. "Take a deep breath. You can smell the coffee brewing and sausage frying. Momma is making gravy, too."

"Get on out of here woman. I've got to find my jeans. The gravy might get cold." He was glad that they had found a familiar, friendly plane again.

"Better start with two biscuits." Mitch handed a basket of bread to Jesse as soon as he was seated. "The other boys ain't one bit bashful and there might not be any left by the time they filter in here and grab a handful to take out to the combines," he teased. "Fine job of getting all that hay done last night. I'm glad to have it in the barn and stacked."

"Oh, I couldn't have done it by myself." Jesse split the biscuits and covered them with steamy, hot sausage gravy. "Lily is an excellent driver and I had to work hard to keep up with her when we were stacking. She uses those hay hooks like she was born with one in each hand," he said.

"Just about was." Mitch Freeman's heart swelled with pride. "She's got some fool notion that she isn't ever going to work on the farm again and it takes a pure act of Kansas congress to get her on a tractor or a hay truck. But she's the best help I ever had. Her old overgrown brothers can do a fair day's work but that Lily . . . now she can put out the steam."

"Hush, Daddy," she giggled. "I only worked hard because my brothers wouldn't let me hear the end of it if they did something better than me."

"I'd say we was smart men, then." Her older brother opened the back door in time to hear what his father said. "You still offering to help in the wheat today?"

"No, he is not." Lily shot a mean look at her brother.

"Well, pardon me," he grinned.

"We're going to plow that field under where the hay was," Lily said. "I'm firing up both the tractors, Daddy. Last time Jesse challenged me to a duel of tractors, I had to make him a peach cobbler because he got finished before I did. Now, we're on my turf and he's going to lose."

"I don't think so." Jesse shook his head. "Once a winner, always a winner. You're a good partner in the business of hay hauling, and you make a mean cobbler. I reckon you could plow a straighter line than anyone I know, but when it comes to production, honey, I can outdo you," he said matter-of-factly.

"How much?" she said, rubbing her thumb across her fingers.

"Elvis," he said.

"Good stakes," she nodded. "You have to bring him to Kansas to live with me if I win. He loves me more than you anyway!"

"Elvis?" her mother asked.

"His big gray tomcat," Lily explained. "Elvis likes me best anyway and he's going to be my cat," she tormented.

"And if I win? What are you putting up for ante?" Jesse teased and everyone waited.

"If you win, Jesse Freeman, which I declare you won't, I'll come to Reagan and make you a peach cobbler," Lily said.

She revved up the tractor motor, put on her earphones, and listened, to Tracy Lawrence singing about the day the good Lord made a woman. She gave Jesse the same thumbs-up sign he gave her that day she lost the race. She'd give him a real race for his money today, but she already knew she'd win, no matter who finished first. Because last night she dreamed that crazy dream about the boat again. Dylan was holding her and then ran off after some other woman. The man in the shadows stepped out and it was Jesse who took her in his arms. Jesse who tilted her head back and looked deep into her blue eyes. When he kissed her the curtains fell on Dylan Reeder, forever blocking him out of her mind as she snuggled into Jesse's chest. A calm peace filled her soul and mended her heart. The wish she'd made on the fairy ring had finally come true.

So she was the winner today, whether she plowed faster and better than Jesse or not. Because Dylan Reeder was gone from her heart . . . forever amen. She'd finally acknowledged that Jesse Freeman was more than just her best friend. It was bittersweet and entirely too late because he was going back to southern Oklahoma tomorrow and he sure didn't feel the same way about her.

Chapter Sixteen

Jesse slept poorly in spite of the weariness in his bones. He'd come to grips with the confusion in his heart. He'd fallen in love with Lily and there was no way around the fact. Somehow in the past several weeks the charade at the family reunion had become reality and now he was in love with a woman who wanted no part of a farm or the farmer who owned it. She'd made that clear enough all summer long and her father had even said so at the breakfast table. And even though she'd been friendly while they plowed all day, it was nothing more than that. Just pure little sister. It was as plain as the clear blue sky that a rumbling turmoil wasn't stirring inside her chest like the one tearing his heart apart at the seams.

He laced his hands under his head and stared out the window at twinkling stars set in a pitch-black sky. It was a crazy world. All summer long she'd been right there every day but even when he realized just touching her brought about a whole fireworks display, she kept calling him Brother Jess. Even when his father teased him about bringing her back home with him, Jesse had shaken his head. Until a tall, preferably blond angel floated past him on a fluffy, white cloud, Jesse wasn't interested in a long-term commitment.

"Not on your life, Dad," he said. "She's a city girl. She understands farm life but she's let me know a million times that she likes her apartment in the city and she hates the farm. Besides she's told me a million times I'm just a big brother. Someone to help her get through a bad time, you know."

"Sister." He sat up and beat his pillow into softness. "Sister!" He repeated as he threw himself backwards on the bed. "Then how did I fall in love with her?"

He hadn't slept more than an hour when the alarm buzzed beside his bed. Five o'clock and he planned to be on the road by five-fifteen. He'd be home before noon and he had a science department meeting at the college at one-thirty. He slipped into a pair of faded jeans and a tee-shirt. The quick motions attested to the fact he was aggravated with himself for falling for a woman who considered him an older brother.

Lily curled up in a recliner in her old bedroom. Tomorrow she was going back to her apartment in town. The second-floor, one-bedroom apartment which had been home since she graduated from college. Her own bed; her own favorite ragged pink towel; her own cheap dishes and dime store forks and knives; her own solitude.

And loneliness.

Why did she fall for Jesse at the last minute? And

how did it happen? It was a rebound thing and she would get over it in a few weeks. Her confused old heart was just hurting and he was there and it happened. Besides, he was a farmer, and she wasn't going to live on a farm the rest of her life. Not even if Elvis did keep her company in the porch swing. Not even if she had wonderful in-laws like the Freemans. It just wasn't worth it. She could fall out of love. She'd managed to do so with Dylan. She'd always be grateful to Jesse for the summer—for the companionship to ease the loneliness, for the camaraderie they'd had, for all the good times. But to condemn herself to a life of pure old farming, forever, amen. No, thank you.

She would simply shut her eyes this minute and tell Jesse good-bye tomorrow morning if she was awake at that time. It was already two in the morning and she was worn completely out from driving a tractor all day so when she finally fell asleep she might not even be awake when he left before the crack of dawn. At three o'clock she left the recliner and went to bed. She lay on her left side so she could look at the moon and stars out the bedroom window. Strange, those were the very same ones she'd beheld that night when she, Jesse, and Elvis watched the sun come up over the trees. The same ones inside the fairy ring the night she stepped on the slug. She shivered at the memory, and then smiled when she remembered how hard Jesse and his folks laughed at the tale on the way to church that morning. At four she paced the floor and argued with herself. There was no way she was ever going to let her heart talk her into admitting to Jesse that she'd actually wanted him to take her in his arms and kiss her for real like he did that day at the reunion when they were pretending.

She was still wearing out the ivory carpet in her bare feet when she heard a door open and close just as gently to avoid waking everyone in the household. He stopped for just a moment at her bedroom door but he didn't knock.

She opened the door and tiptoed a few feet behind him to the front door. "Ready to go?" She hugged her electric blue kimono-style robe around her body.

He jumped. "Yep, got miles to go and things to do." He smiled that lopsided grin and she almost threw caution to the wind and herself into his arms.

"Well, thanks for everything, Jesse," she said, but she didn't cross the acres between them even though her heart was pounding. "Thanks for getting me the job, rescuing me out of the depression, and for all the good times. Even for stacking hay and . . ." She searched his face but there wasn't anything there to give her hope that he'd had a change of heart through the night. "I'm sorry I doubted your story. I was just so mad . . ."

"No apologies or thanks necessary," he said. "You pulled your own weight in every circumstance, Lily. Have a good school year and keep in touch." He wanted to reach out and touch her, to draw her to his chest in a hug that didn't have a bit of sisterly affection in it. But she didn't take a single step forward to let him know there was a possibility she had changed her mind about farm life or him.

"Well, good-bye, and drive carefully, and bring me Elvis. I beat you fair and square," she said.

"Elvis would die in an apartment where he couldn't

roam the pastures and bring in a field mouse every day or so. And you know it, Lily." He wanted to add if she wanted the cat she needed to rethink the way she felt about farms.

"Oh, I know it, but . . ."

"But what, Lily?" His heart stopped for a minute.

"Oh, nothing." She managed a smile. "I really don't like good-byes. Especially when it's to a good friend and a big brother."

"I see." His heart dropped. So that was still the way she felt. Well, then it was home to the farm and Elvis. Home to Marcy coming back in a few weeks and his parents. To a new school year with new students and a big old gaping hole in his chest where his heart used to be. And he'd get over it . . . but he sure didn't have to like it.

Chapter Seventeen

Lily got right back into her teaching routine with gusto. She encouraged her track girls, baited them, fussed at them, listened to their problems, and endured a million questions about why she was still Coach Winslow and hadn't gotten married that summer. The first three weeks she checked her answering machine every day for a call from Jesse. Maybe a joke or some news about Elvis.

But it was never there.

She got a long letter from Marcy the week after she got back to Coffeyville. She and Jacob had been offered a position in Russia for a semester, a teaching–learning experience, and the college in Tishomingo had agreed to work with them. Marcy mentioned that Jesse had phoned a couple of times. The phone lines were horrid at best and they hadn't talked long, but he seemed busy with the new semester. Her letter was filled with all the new things she and Jacob were experiencing and hopes that Lily had gotten over the terrible situation with Dylan. And when Lily wrote her, she told her about school, the wheat harvest, and assured and reassured her that Dylan Reeder was history, and in this instance, history which did not repeat itself.

Fall finally replaced the summer heat. The leaves turned from green to dark amber, brilliant yellow and deep burgundy, but her heart didn't turn. It missed Jesse. It wanted to hear his voice on the phone, or make an excuse to drive to Oklahoma and see him. Down deep she knew it was more just missing Jesse's friendship and there wasn't one bit of sense in starting something that couldn't be finished. Besides, just because her deranged, stupid heart changed horses in the middle of the stream didn't mean Jesse felt anything but what he declared . . . that she was just like a sister to him.

She was reading the newest Sue Grafton mystery one night when the phone rang. *Jesse!* She thought for the gajillionth time in two months.

"Hello," she said breathlessly.

"Lily?" a deep male voice asked and her heart stopped in the middle of a beat.

"Yes," she managed to whisper.

"This is Barry Patterson," he said.

She could have cried. Not tears of joy but pure, unadulterated disappointment. The way the new assistant football coach said her name had almost the same inflection as Jesse used. But then Barry was from north Texas and had a drawl not totally unlike Jesse's. "Well, what can I do for you?" she tried to be friendly.

"You can go out to dinner with me tomorrow night," he said.

"Oh." She tried to think up a reason she couldn't go. She had to wash her hair, finish reading her book, anything.

"Is that a yes or no?" he asked.

"It's a yes," she said. She was never going to get over Jesse if she didn't make an effort. "I'd love to go to dinner with you."

"Good, I'll pick you up at six then," he said.

"I'll be ready," she told him. And she would be. At least on the outside.

Barry had dark hair and green eyes. He was only slightly overweight and just a few inches taller than Lily. He dressed in casual khaki slacks and a navy-blue knit shirt and his shaving lotion was spicy and pleasant. But none of it tickled her hormones or kicked up her sass.

"So what brought you to Coffeyville?" she asked as they waited for their steaks.

"A job. A starting point," he said. "I coached junior high in Grapevine for three years. This is a step up the ladder. What brought you to Coffeyville?"

"It's home," she said. But was it really? Seemed like the past summer she'd questioned every single answer she gave.

"Did you go to school this summer or just be a lazy old teacher?" he asked.

"Oh, I spent the summer in southern Oklahoma. Little bitty dot on the map called Reagan. I was house-sitting for my friend who's in Russia doing a little teaching–learning over there. Her brother got me a job at the local ju-co down there for the summer. I really liked working with that age group." Conversation was getting easier.

"That's my next step. A ju-co and then university," he said.

"Jesse, that's my friend's brother, teaches at the ju-co. He's a math teacher and does farming on the side. They didn't have football there, but they did play some basketball. Jesse and I became really good friends over the summer." She sipped her tea.

"I thought about basketball one time, but it's just not me," he said with a long, lingering look over the table. She wondered if it was supposed to relay some kind of primal message that would make her kick off her shoes. If she was supposed to jerk the tablecloth off and grab him by the shirt collar and drag him up on the table for a quick moment of passion. If it was, it didn't work.

"Well, Jesse likes the ju-co level. I guess he could go on to a university but he says he's found his place in the sun right where he is," she rambled.

"My place in the sun is big bucks." Barry smiled and a chunk of tomato from the pre-dinner salad was stuck between his teeth.

"There's more important things than money in life," she said. And what are they? Another question for her to worry over like one of her dad's hound dogs with a bone. They are contentment, trust, love, sharing life with someone like Jesse—she answered that one in a hurry and went on to think about each item she'd just listed while Barry told a story about a friend of his in Texas.

"And then I said to him . . . there might be more important things than money, but if there is, please don't tell me right now," Barry was saying when she tuned back into the conversation.

It was downhill from there. Every time he said something she thought of Jesse. Every gesture reminded her of an opposite one . . . Jesse's. The date wasn't doing one thing to ease the hole Jesse left in her life when he walked out the door. It was just making the edges more raw than they'd been in weeks.

Finally she let him talk and she nodded occasionally so he wouldn't think she'd died and call the undertaker to cart her carcass off to the nearest funeral parlor. But mostly she tried to deal with the realization that she was sorting out her feelings while she was out on a full-fledged date with another man. What she'd felt for Dylan was just pure infatuation. If he'd been faithful it might have developed into something other than that, but he wasn't and it was water under the bridge. What she had and felt with her Jesse was something deeper and more lasting. It was the love that kept couples together until their golden wedding anniversary. And that's why it was so hard to get over it.

Barry walked her to the apartment door, put his palms on the door to capture her in the circle. She was quieter when it was a one-on-one situation. In the teacher's lounge she was animated and lively. But then he probably overwhelmed her with this outgoing personality.

He leaned down to kiss her and she turned her cheek. "Thanks for a wonderful dinner." She turned quickly and unlocked her apartment door.

"How about a cup of coffee to finish it off?" He brushed her hair back and strung a series of wet kisses across her neck.

"Not tonight." She opened the door.

"I'll call you tomorrow," he told her.

But he didn't and she was glad.

The phone rang a week later when she was in the middle of grading papers for the history class they'd asked her to teach that semester. "I don't want to talk to Barry," she muttered on the sixth ring as she reached across the sofa for the phone. Even though he hadn't called, there'd been these long, puppy-dog looks when she met him in the halls. They were supposed to make her knees weak and her body melt in a puddle at his feet. They just made her angry.

"Lily?" he said when she answered the phone. "This is Jesse Freeman down here in Reagan, Oklahoma."

"Jesse, is it really you?" she said breathlessly. "I'm so glad to hear your voice. How's Marcy and your folks? And Elvis? Does he miss me? And did you get the hay all in before those rains hit down there? I read about it in the paper and saw the news."

"Hey, slow down. We can talk all night if we want. We don't have to hurry," he laughed. "Marcy and Jacob will be back in the states just before Christmas, which they plan to spend in Texas with his folks. Then they'll be here for New Year's with us. Elvis is moping because I didn't bring you back to him. I got all the hay in and we didn't get the flood they predicted."

"Gosh, it's good to hear your voice. I thought you'd just gone home and forgot all about me," she admitted honestly. "And fall courses? Did the teacher I replaced come back? Tell me everything," she begged.

"Teacher came back. Fall courses are routine and I didn't forget you, Lily. I remembered you every time I sunk my hay hooks into a bale. I didn't have anyone to help me unload hay. Looks like you could have had pity on this poor old farmer and come on down here a couple of weekends and helped me out like I did you?"

"I wasn't invited," she snapped impatiently.

"Like I told you about the house that night. We don't stand on invitations when we're family," he reminded her.

Family, her mind screamed. *So I'm still just a sister. Well, Jesse I can't get you off my mind or out of my heart, and you still feel like I'm your sister. Life is sure full of twists and turns, isn't it?*

"You still there Lily?" he asked. *Women.* One minute she was excited just to hear his voice and actually made him wonder if she might have missed him. The next she was as silent as a cold, dark tomb.

"Sure, I'm here," she said but all the warmth was gone from her voice.

"Well, what did I say wrong?" he asked gruffly and she giggled.

"Not one thing, Jesse. So don't you get on a high horse," she snapped. "What did you call for anyway?"

"Touchy, ain't we?" he said right back. "I called to see what you're doing over fall break next week. Thought maybe you might like to come down and visit Elvis. You do have visitation rights, you know. You won fair and square."

"Got a better idea. Bring him to visit me. We've got a harvest party on Friday night and you can go with me," she said. "We'll dance and eat barbecue and bring Elvis some . . ."

"Elvis doesn't ride well. Have to give him pills before I take him to the vet for his shots every year. Am I invited without him?"

"I suppose," she sighed.

"Hey, does that mean you'd rather see Elvis than me?"

"It doesn't matter what it means. Can you come?"

"I'll be there with my dancin' boots on and ready to . . . oh, I forgot, I do have to be in the area that weekend. At least Saturday night and Sunday. When's your harvest party? I figured if you came down here you and Momma could do something while I attended a couple of meetings."

"Friday night. You could come on Friday and go back Saturday afternoon . . . but if you can't make it . . ." she started.

"I didn't say that. I'll be there. Matter of fact I'll be there on Thursday night. There's no classes Thursday or Friday at the college," he said through clenched teeth. Mercy, but she had a way of making him want to bite ten penny nails. He'd worked hard these past months but the visions of Lily wouldn't leave him, not in waking minutes or in dreams. He knew she wasn't one bit interested in his way of life but that didn't keep him from picking up the phone almost nightly and dialing her number, only to hang up before it even rang one time.

Tonight he was so excited to finally work up the nerve to call her with an invitation to come back to Reagan during fall break and then he'd practically lost his courage when he dialed the number. Why start something they couldn't or wouldn't finish? Even though she was the best help he'd ever had, farming wasn't something she wanted to devote her life to. The tone of her voice had just made that even clearer than he remembered. Well, he was going to Coffeyville and maybe after his stupid heart realized that she wasn't available, then it would quit aching for her all the time.

Chapter Eighteen

Lily waited on the front porch. Jesse should be there any moment if she'd gauged the time right and she wasn't skirting around the issue another minute. When he got out of the truck she was hitting him with the whole ball of wax right in the chest, and if he didn't like what she had to say he could go back to Reagan.

This time for good.

Jesse turned off the headlights and sat in the truck just a minute more. He hoped she answered the door when he knocked because things were about to come to a head. Right then. If she stood there on the porch and told him he was her surrogate big brother, then he was going to state his piece and drive right back to Reagan.

This time for good.

He started around the bed of the truck and she stepped off the porch. Both of them stopped for a moment when they saw each other. He was still in shadows and she was barely illuminated by the dim porch light.

"Lily?" he whispered. She was beautiful in a pair of faded jeans, her sock feet, and a Halloween sweatshirt with a ghost on the front.

"Jesse?" she whispered back. Her breath caught in a gasp just looking at him.

"I am not your sister," she declared.

"Well, I'm not your brother," he told her.

They met somewhere in the middle of the yard in a fierce embrace. He tilted her chin back and nothing had ever felt as good as the calluses on his palms next to her skin. She tiptoed and when his lips touched hers it was even more breathtaking than the kiss they'd shared at the reunion. That one was pretend and this was as real as the stars twinkling in the sky above them on a nippy fall night. No one had ever made her insides turn to a bowl of heated mush with just a kiss before. She wanted it to go on and on.

"Wow, If I'd known this kind of affection was waiting for me I would've been here sooner," he whispered in her ear.

"Oh, then I'm for sure not your sister anymore?" she looked at him quizzically.

"No, ma'am. Never were. Still can't imagine why you ever thought that," he shook his head.

"Because you said so," she told him bluntly.

"Well, you kept calling me *brother* Jesse," he said in the same tone.

"Are we fighting already?" she asked.

"Probably, but if we are it's a lover's spat and not sibling rivalry, and that's a fact." He drew her close for another kiss.

* * *

Lily laid out her western clothing carefully on Friday night. She remembered the time Dylan told her if she wanted to attend foolish harvest dances, she'd have to do it without him. He didn't want their apartment cluttered with a bunch of hick clothing because he wasn't going to a country bumpkin affair where he wasn't comfortable. So she'd taken her dress jeans and western cut shirts to her old bedroom at her folks' farm.

It was as if she'd opened the doors to the home of an old friend when she fingered the stiffly starched jeans. She chose a pair of deep, dark green ones with side chaps and her lace-up Ropers to match. Then she picked out a long-sleeved shirt of a lighter green, with a triangle-shaped cut-out right below the button on the high collar. She fastened on a thin, gold chain with her initials on the drop around her neck. She held the charm up and sprayed a mist of perfume across the two inches of healthy cleavage showing in the cut-out.

"Now, we'll see if Jesse Freeman can dance as well as he can plow." She checked the vision in the mirror on the back of her bedroom door. "Oops," she tiptoed up to the top hanger on the hall tree just to the side of the door and picked up her ecru dress hat with the dark green hat band. "That finishes it off," she nodded to the reflection. "Go have a good time, Lily Marie Winslow. And make Jesse dance until his feet hurt for not bringing Elvis to you. I'm sure that cat is terribly disappointed because he can't come live with you . . . so I guess you'll just have to go live with him," she giggled.

"Whoooooeee," Mitch whistled through his teeth

when his daughter waltzed into the living room. "Looks like my daughter has really come home. Haven't seen you look that classy in ages," he grinned. "Momma, come and look at Lily."

June peeped around the door. "Pretty good get-up," she smiled. "Have you seen Jesse? You better chase out to the barn and get you a pair of brass knucks down from the wall. That boy is going to start a fight tonight amongst the women. And you may have to fight off the hussies to keep him. If that sassy Vivien Hollister don't try to sneak him out from under you, I'll be willing to eat my hat."

"Who does he remind you of?" Lily asked.

"Why, if his hair was a little lighter and his eyes weren't so dark, he'd be a dead ringer for James Dean," her mother said. "If you decide you don't want to brand him, I betcha there'll be a waiting line a mile long tonight," she said. "He's waiting on the porch swing. Get on out there. Don't waste much time, girl. He's a keeper. Hard worker. Handsome enough that if I was thirty years younger I'd pitch your dad out in the yard and let him park his boots under my bed."

"Here now. That's enough of that foul-mouthed talk." Mitch shook his finger but grinned all the same.

"Thanks, Momma," Lily said.

Jesse's heart stopped in the middle of a beat when she stepped out the front door. He eyed her from the toes of her green Ropers to the ecru hat covering part of her delightfully curly hair, and he was lost forever. This was the woman he wanted to spend the rest of his life with, and if he had to fight her aversion to the farm and every cowpoke in southern Kansas to claim her, then he was up to the task.

"You are simply beautiful." He crossed the porch, the heels of his dress boots making a sound she'd never forget because it would always remind her of the night they met halfway and the whole world stood still for them. The night when it suddenly didn't matter if he was a farmer or if she had to haul hay, talk about new baby calves, or cook supper every night for a man with specks of dirt still sticking to his hair. It didn't matter what she had to do if she could convince Jesse Freeman that she was in desperately in love with him.

"And you, Jesse, are pretty handsome, yourself." She wrapped her arms around his neck. "Momma says the women will flock around you like flies on the honey jar," she whispered.

"But I won't see them." He wanted to do more than just hold her. "Not a single one as long as you're there."

The party was in full swing when Jesse and Lily walked through the big doors at the north end of the barn. The floor had been swept until it was spotless. Flames from hurricane lamps, set in the middle of tables, flickered and the smell of good barbecue permeated the whole barn.

A red-haired woman with a top-heavy figure waved from across the barn and before Lily could blink, Vivien Hollister was at her fingertips. "I'm glad you're here. I was afraid you'd call with some weak excuse." She hugged Lily briefly. "And who is this handsome creature you've brought with you?" She eyed Jesse from top to bottom and back down again like she'd like to have him for supper . . . and possibly breakfast, too.

"Jesse, this is Vivien Hollister, daughter of the man

who owns this place. She's been my friend since grade school," Lily said. "And this is Jesse Freeman, Vivien. I told you about him when I came back from Reagan. The man who helped me make it through the summer."

"Are there any more like him down in Oklahoma?" She didn't take her eyes from his face and he blushed.

"Wouldn't know. You'll have to go spend a summer down there and see if you can find one for yourself," Lily said. "Jesse, dance with me." She took his hand and led him to the dance floor.

"If she doesn't treat you right, I'll be in the wings," Vivien laughed and waved.

"I don't think so." Lily shook her head.

Jesse took her in his arms, pulled her close to his chest, liking the way she fit there so naturally. "But what if I like the way she fills out that tight blouse?" he teased as they started a slow waltz around the dance floor.

"Like anything you want," Lily said. "But remember two things tonight, Jesse Freeman. I am not your sister and I do not want to be kin to you in any sense of the word. And the second thing is that I do not share, so if you're not through shopping, then you can't play with my toys."

"Yes, ma'am," he said with a sexy grin.

Dylan didn't want to go to a silly, backwoods barn dance. He hated those things. Dancing was fine but its place was in a ballroom after dinner, with nice soft music and refined people. He didn't care if Rachel said the barn was swept clean of hay. If there was a bale within two miles, he'd start sneezing by the time he'd been there ten minutes.

"I'm going, and you're going with me," Rachel declared. "I know you don't own a pair of good tight Wranglers, much less a western shirt, but you can wear a pair of casual slacks and a knit shirt. If I can go to that faculty dinner then you can sure go with me to the Hollister harvest dance."

"But isn't that the farm next to where Lily's folks live?" he asked.

"Yes, it is, and they might even be there, but you're going with me even if she's there with them. You're not hiding out forever from those folks. You should have stood up to her anyway when we started seeing each other again, Dylan, and you know it," Rachel said.

"I didn't see you jumping out of your purple maid-of-honor dress and telling her anything," he retorted.

"No, I didn't," Rachel said. "But it's all water under the bridge now and we're going to this dance."

Dylan agreed but he pouted the whole time he dressed. An hour, that's all. He was leaving in an hour and if Rachel wanted to stay until dawn and dance with every tobacco-dipping, redneck there, then he'd leave her there and she could find her own way home. If this was the price he had to pay for her to go with him to a civilized party then he would never take her with him again.

Rachel wore tight blue jeans, white boots, and a white lace, western cut blouse with flowing sleeves, caught up with a satin cuff. And a satin teddy underneath. She did look good, Dylan had to admit as she looped her arm in his as they walked through the darkness toward the lights of the barn. When they stepped inside the doors, she caught sight of Vivien next to the bandstand and told Dylan over the top of the noise and music that she would be right back. He didn't hear her say a word or know that she was gone because the first thing he saw when his eyes adjusted to the light was Lily in the middle of the dance floor. She was leaning back, looking up into a strange man's face and smiling brightly. His hands were on her waist and hers were looped loosely around his neck. The way the man looked at her made Dylan want to stomp and cuss.

He almost left right then but Vivien and Rachel were beside him, mumbling and talking about Lily bringing her new love to the dance that night. There wasn't anything for him to do but go with them to a table where he continued to watch the dancing couple from a distance. She'd never looked at him like she was looking at this Jesse Freeman . . . at least that's the name he caught in passing when Vivien whispered excitedly to Rachel. The way Lily's eyes sparkled as she looked at Jesse's face was enough to deflate Dylan's ego into a pile of mush. He didn't even deserve a good cursing from Lily after the stunt he'd pulled, but he never, ever expected to be in the same room with her again. Much less have to watch her dance with another man.

When he slipped out the back door of the church that night in May and saw Lily get into a car belonging to one of the bridesmaids . . . the one from Oklahoma . . . and disappear, he'd sighed with relief. He'd loved her, or at least he thought he did, and then Rachel was back in the picture and he didn't really know how to get out of the situation with either of them. A few days went by, and Rachel ingrained herself back into his life. Still yet, he still awoke in the middle of the night with his arms aching for Lily.

Lily smiled brightly at something Jesse said and then he held her even tighter, and Dylan's nerves twisted into a knot of pain. He'd made the wrong choice and it was too late to change it now. Lily was out of his reach and never could be his again. But just in case he was wrong, he determined he would swallow his foolish pride, apologize, and beg for another chance.

"Handsome, ain't he?" Vivien was saying to Rachel.

"I can't believe she brought him to this dance. I've never missed a Hollister harvest party, and she knew I'd bring Dylan," Rachel snapped. "I don't care if he looks like a movie star, she doesn't have any business wrecking my night."

"She hasn't ever missed one of my parties either," Vivien snapped right back. "And if she wrecks a lot of parties for you, Rachel, it won't repay you for the night you wrecked her life, will it?" Vivien reminded her bluntly. "If you start anything tonight, honey, I'll finish it. So you better be good."

"Where are *you* going?" Rachel asked Dylan as he started to the middle of the dance floor.

"I'm dancing with Lily if she'll let me, and you can like it or not," he said.

"Over my dead body." Rachel stood up fast enough to knock the folding chair backwards. "You're not going to even speak to her."

"I owe her more than a dance," Dylan said. "I owe

her an apology, and I'm delivering it now. And you're going to sit down and shut up," he said calmly.

"Excuse me." Dylan tapped Jesse on the shoulder.

Jesse felt Lily stiffen and saw the anger in her eyes.

"What are you doing here, Dylan?" Lily asked.

"Asking for a dance with you?" Dylan smiled and hoped to see that adoration in her eyes he'd seen before.

"I'll find us something to drink." Jesse brushed a quick kiss across her lips. He was wise enough to know that she'd best take care of any past business. Because when Lily looked up at him he didn't want there to be a flicker of doubt in her eyes. All he wanted to see was love for Jesse Freeman.

"What do you want?" She put her hand on his shoulder and held out her hand for him to take it in a more formal dance than she'd been enjoying with Jesse. "If I remember correctly, you wouldn't ever waste your time in a hick hoe-down like this. You didn't like my western-cut clothes or anything to do with this life."

"You're right, and I was wrong," he said simply. "I owe you more than an apology, but it's all I have to give." He stopped in the middle of the dance and tilted her chin up to look into her eyes. "Come outside with me, so we can talk in private."

"All right," she nodded, unaware that Rachel was literally biting her nails on one side of the barn, and Jesse was keeping an eye on them from the other side. Watching her follow Dylan outside was the most difficult thing Jesse ever did; sitting still was the next hardest.

"Okay, now what have you got to say that you want

to do it in private?" Lily backed up against Jesse's truck for support.

"I threw away the most wonderful thing in the world, Lily," Dylan said smoothly. "When I saw you with that redneck I realized I was wrong. Give me another chance? This isn't where you belong. You've told me a hundred times, you'd never marry a farmer, and that man in there is as hick as they come." He reached to put his arm around her and let his thumb travel down the length of her ribcage.

Lily picked his hand up and dropped it like it was dirty trash. "Don't touch me."

Dylan sneered. "Why did you come out here with me if you didn't care?"

"To flush you out of my life forever," she said bluntly. "There isn't time, chance, or place for me to get involved with you again. I'd be a bitter old maid and I'd still never give you another chance, Dylan. Relationships are built on trust, and there isn't any of that left between us. You destroyed it."

"I see." His tone turned icy. "Well, please accept my apologies. I should have told you about Rachel when you mentioned her name. I'm sorry about the whole mess."

"You don't see, Dylan," Lily said, "and you feel even less. What did you think you were doing to my heart when you promised Rachel you'd spend the weekend after our honeymoon with her and that you'd file for divorce? You were thinking about going to bed with her while you were standing in front of my folks, your parents, and even God about to make your wedding vows. So you don't see anything."

"I said I was sorry. I'm going back in and get Rachel and we're going home," he said bluntly.

"You live with her and you're trying to talk me into a second chance?" Lily could hardly believe what she was hearing.

"Well, you came here with someone else and you're out here listening to me, so where does that leave you?" he said.

"Dylan, you are the biggest mistake I ever made. My heart doesn't have any eyes or ears. So it depended on me to see and to hear. But I was blind and deaf when it came to you, and pretty stupid, too. But there's someone in my life now that our hearts blend so well together we don't need to see or hear. And I could trust Jesse to the ends of eternity. I wouldn't ever have to wonder where he was if he worked late. I don't know what I'm doing out here with you because he's in there and that's where my heart is. Right beside his. You know, I really wanted to tell you off. I wanted to cuss and rant and rave and pitch a hissy fit to get rid of the anger inside me. But right now, I just feel sorry for you. Sorry that you're a selfish rogue, and you'll never know what it's like to love someone enough to give them your whole heart with no reservations. Sorry that you're never going to know the contentment and peace I have found in Jesse's arms. Go home with Rachel. I think you two are cut from the same bolt of cloth and deserve each other."

"You're living in a fantasy world." He turned away from her just in time to run into Rachel.

"Maybe so," Lily said, "probably so. And I love it so much I've going to live here forever," she laughed.

"Hello, Rachel. You're looking good. White was always good on you."

"Let's go home, Dylan." She grabbed his arm possessively. "Stay away from us, Lily. Don't drag him outside again or you're going to deal with me."

"Better keep a close eye on your investment, there," Lily said to Rachel. "The stock market might fall someday and you'll find you're holding a whole lifetime of nothing but worthless paper. Stay for the party. Don't go rushing off on my account. I don't want him. He's all yours, sweetheart. Good luck."

She checked her reflection in the mirror on Jesse's truck by the light of the moon. The girl she saw staring back had a new sparkle in her eyes, a new smile on her face, and a new determination written all over her face. She shut her eyes tightly and the only face there was Jesse Freeman's.

If there was ever another incident with Amber, she wasn't throwing out a whole pan of cinnamon rolls and running away. She was going to bow right up to that brazen hussy and fight for Jesse, because anything worth having was worth taking a stand for. No more confusion. No more bewilderment. Just a straight course from her heart to his. She set her feet firmly to run the course with determination.

She worked hard to conjure up a vision of Dylan in his white tennis shorts, his blond hair picking up the sun rays and a few sweat beads glowing on his upper lip. Nothing. Not even a faint picture in the shadows of her mind. He was inside the barn, probably dancing with Rachel and tossing back bottled water, closer than he'd been since the night she called off the wedding. And yet he was so far removed from her that he could have been sitting in the North Pole having coffee with Santa Claus.

She opened the door and located Jesse. Two cans of Dr. Pepper were in front of him, waiting for her to come and claim one of them—along with his heart.

"Lily." Vivien was at her elbow. "I saw you go outside with Dylan. You're not entertaining notions of that, are you? Good heavens, girl, he wouldn't be faithful to anyone. Rachel is just livid. She knows she was a hussy, but she won't ever admit it."

"No, Vivien, we were just clearing the air. I needed to do that much so I can get on with life. Jesse is waiting for me," Lily said.

"You're both my friends. But just because Rachel is my friend doesn't mean what she did was right. And if you get tired of that hunk you brought in here, kick him across the fence to me. Just looking at those broody eyes gives me hot flashes." Vivien fanned her face with the back of her hand.

"I don't think so," Lily laughed. "I think I'll keep him."

"Hello." She sat down on Jesse's knee and picked up one of the cans. "Thanks for getting me something to drink. You about ready to dance again?"

"Lily." Her mother appeared at the table. "You better get Jesse on the dance floor. I saw Vivien with a covetous look in her eyes."

"Thou shalt not covet thy neighbor's ox," Lily intoned dramatically. "Or thy best friend's feller, either. Come on Jesse. Dance with me." She took his hand and dragged him to the middle of the floor.

He wrapped his arms around her waist. She looped both her arms around his neck and leaned back and really looked at Jesse Freeman. She saw a man who could be trusted forever.

"Is it over?" he asked as he moved gracefully into a slow two-step.

"It's over," she nodded.

"Am I going to find him sneaking in your bedroom when I bring you breakfast in bed?" Jesse laughed.

She snorted and giggled at the same time.

"Want to go outside with me?"

"What brought that on?" she asked.

"Well, you stopped and looked up at him like this while ago and then you went outside with him," Jesse reminded her. "And I waited patiently for him to have his turn. Of course, I was scared to death that you'd come back in holding his hand and looking at him with your big, blue beautiful eyes and tell me you'd decided to give him another chance and all those kisses we've shared since last night weren't for real."

"Were you really?" she asked.

"Yes, Lily, I was, and I realized how much you mean to me, and I was prepared to fight or beg, whichever it took to keep you," he admitted honestly.

"I'm not going outside with you." She said. "Want to know why?"

"Why?"

"Because what we've got will stand up under the lights and right out in public for anyone to see, forever. It's over with Dylan. And honey, I'm ready for a new relationship . . . with you." She tiptoed to brush a kiss across his lips. "And I sure don't mean a sisterly one either," she said.

"Well, you sure didn't want to be anything more all summer," he retorted. "And I think your words were that you couldn't wait to get back to the city and away from the farm."

"Are we fighting again, Jesse?" she smiled, her eyes twinkling.

"Maybe, but we can make up later." He started dancing again, lifting her feet off the floor and dancing with her like he would a child. "I'm a farmer, Lily. I can't change what I am, and I know you don't want that kind of life so maybe we better slow this buggy down and consider everything."

"I thought I didn't," she said. "But somewhere in the midst of everything, I forgot to tell my heart that. This is life, Jesse. Dancing with you at the harvest dance. Plowing the fields with you. Stacking hay with you. Life is that, Jesse . . . with you. That's what makes it life. And I'm ready to jump into it with both eyes wide open."

"I want a repeat right now, Lily. Tell me one more time about life being with me. I like that part . . . with me. And while you're at it, could you tell me exactly what we're going to do about us?"

She opened her eyes and there was Dylan staring right at her from across the room. Rachel was fussing at him about something, but his eyes were on Jesse dancing her around with her feet off the ground. She burrowed down deeper in his shoulder. He swirled her around twice and the song ended. Just to make sure, she shut her eyes again. And the only person there was her precious Jesse.

"Right now we're going to dance and look deeply into each other's eyes, and fall in love just like in the storybooks. And someday we'll ride off into the sunset together," she whispered.

He kissed her briefly on the lips in the middle of the dance floor but it held the promise of something more . . . later.

Chapter Nineteen

Jesse thought about proposing on Christmas Day in Kansas, but his romantic side wanted something more. Maybe on New Year's Eve they'd drive down to the park in Tishomingo where they'd had lunch during the summer. He'd tie her engagement ring to a long-stemmed red rose. Maybe a big square solitaire on a gold band. And at the stroke of midnight he'd ask her to marry him. Start off the brand-new year with the right question, hopefully the right answer, and the right woman to spend his whole life with.

She'd declared she didn't want a big white church wedding again but she might want a simple affair at the Freeman farm. Jesse didn't care if they got married in blue jeans out in the middle of the pasture, just so long as it was legal, binding, and forever. He didn't care if one person or sixty thousand heard him say his vows. He was saying them for Lily, anyway, not a crowd of people. Just a few simple words . . . the same words already written deep in his heart.

"Pretty quiet." She slid across the pickup seat and kissed his earlobe. "What are you thinking about?"

"I enjoyed the party last night." He could avoid the question but not the heat her kisses caused. "Fine people. I like your family a lot," he said in short, quipped sentences that still took most of his breath.

"They liked you, too. Momma said you're a keeper."

Jesse smiled that crooked James Dean grin she loved. "Funny. That's the same thing Daddy said about you. What are we going to do about us, Lily?"

"I think maybe we'd better plan on me moving." She laid her head on his shoulder.

"You'd move?" His heavy heart floated.

"I've just plumb fallen in love with you, Jesse. So I'm interested in staying in southern Oklahoma . . . because that's where you are. I like teaching but I've also learned to love the Freeman farm, believe it or not. And I'm tired of these long weekend drives. If a small school . . . Mill Creek, Tishomingo, Wapanucka, or even Ardmore needs a coach, I'd commute. Or I might not even have to work at all if I could find an old dirt farmer to support me," she said sleepily. "But for right now, can I sleep right here on your shoulder? Maybe I'll put in some applications this week," she said, already shutting her eyes. "Think we'll have a white Christmas after all even if it is a couple of days late?"

"Never know," he said but she was already asleep.

Not even in today's permissive world would Jesse

ask her to move in with him, even if they were two grown adults and he wanted more than those steamy, sexy goodnight kisses which practically made him pant with desire. He would give her a courtship complete with a rehearsal dinner—after which he would most certainly not go straight to the maid of honor's arms. He'd even be willing for big wedding with every Freeman who could drive to Coffeyville, and a honeymoon to the moon if he could book a rocket going that way. All that would take several months, but he'd waited forever for the right woman. Six months wasn't any big thing. He'd wait six years if necessary to be able to carry her over the threshold to his house to live with him forever.

She slept an hour, then wiggled until she woke herself up. "Where are we?" She yawned and tried to get her bearings. "How much farther?"

"We're on the outskirts of Tulsa," he said. "Another three hours. Maybe more."

"Look Jesse, it's snowing. Real flakes. We're going to have a white Christmas at the farm." She pointed to the windshield.

The snow continued to fall in big gorgeous flakes the rest of the way to Reagan. When they parked the truck in the front yard at the farm she jumped out of the truck and began catching them on her tongue like a child. "Oh, Jesse, isn't it wonderful. I may stand out here all day just so I won't miss a minute of it."

He leaned against the cold door of the pickup truck and watched Lily dancing with her denim duster flowing around her as she twisted and turned. "Didn't know you were a ballerina?" He wrapped his arms around her and drew her close for a passionate kiss.

"I took it from the time I was six all the way through high school, but you don't do ballet, so we'll compromise." She wrapped her arms around his neck and started to sway. "We'll two-step in the snow." She started singing her own country rendition of "You Light Up My Life."

"Thank you for a lovely dance, kind sir." She bowed gracefully when she ended the song.

"My pleasure, ma'am." He tipped his western hat.

"I think we better go inside but I hate to leave. Can we come back out after dinner and presents?"

"Anything you want," he laughed. "Here come the rest of the crew, so we'd better unload these suitcases and get ready for the onslaught. Everyone is so excited that you are here. I may not get a word in edgewise."

"How'd the weekend go?" Mitch asked after they'd opened presents.

"Great," Jesse said. "The whole family was there. There's more of them than the Freeman family reunion. It's noisy and wonderful."

"Thought y'all might get here last night?" Marcy beamed. They were the perfect couple. Jesse had love written all over his face and oozing out his pores, and love was dancing out of Lily's eyes. She would have never dared to hope that the summer would net profits like it had, but she was sure happy with the results of bringing Lily to Reagan to heal her broken heart after that disastrous wedding night.

"Oh, we decided to get up early and drive down this morning," Lily said but she couldn't hide the high color in her cheeks. "We had a family to-do last night."

"I can't believe you two are really dating?" Marcy

laughed. "Go away for six months and look what happens."

"Reckon we ought to kidnap Lily and not let her go back?" Mitch said.

"I'm trying to, Dad." Jesse sat down on the sofa and drew her down to sit closely beside him.

"Well, you better try harder. Way she can handle a hay hook and way she can sing, not to mention all those cooking skills, you might need to put a little more effort into it," Mitch said.

"That's right." She cocked her head to one side and looked right into his eyes. "And besides all that I can plow straighter than you can."

"Yeah, but not as much. I can outplow you when it comes to production." He picked up her hand and kissed her fingertips.

"Only because I let you." She laughed and pulled her hand away. "If I really wanted to I could beat you."

"Bull," he snorted. "I beat you fair and square."

"Children, children," June laughed. "No fighting at the dinner table."

"But Momma," Jesse looked confused, "you always said when you and Daddy fight, it's so you can make up later," he said then roared in laughter at her blushing face.

Later that night, Lily heard him open the door carefully and slip down the hallway to the bedroom and she held her breath. There was no way he was crawling into her bed with his parents asleep in the room right next door. Not in this house or even in his. Not until they were really married. And Jesse hadn't said a thing about marriage yet.

"Lily," he whispered.

"I'm awake. Turn on the light, Jesse," she said.

"Why? I just came to see if you want to go outside and sit in the porch swing. I can't sleep, darlin'," he whispered.

"Just do it," she said. "Please, Jesse."

He reached for the switch and the room lit up. "Now sit down beside me." She patted the bed. "I hesitate to do this but I'm not sneaking around, or playing dumb while your parents wink at each other while we sit on the sofa holding hands like teenagers. So, Jesse Freeman, will you marry me?"

If the artificial light hadn't lit up the room, his face would have done it. "I thought I needed to court you forever and then we'd have a big, white wedding at your folks' house," he whispered.

"I don't care anything about a wedding. I just want to be your wife." She sat up straight and kissed him, running her tongue over his lower lip until he opened his mouth and moaned.

"Then, Lily Winslow, I will be honored to be your husband," he whispered into her dark hair. "And I'll give you six hours to stop molesting me. Let's see, there'll be a cold day in July or something about St. Peter selling snowcones somewhere about seven times hotter than an Oklahoma summer when you . . ."

"You're incorrigible," she giggled.

"When are we getting married? Maybe in our house, since you don't want a big wedding?" He kissed her between words.

"On January second. That's next week. I'm calling

the superintendent tomorrow and telling him I'm faxing my resignation. My assistant coach will think she's got the biggest Christmas present in the world if they'll let her take over my position. We could wait until my school year is finished, but I can't live for five months on kisses and raging hormones. Besides when summer comes we'll be so busy on the farm we won't have time for long, lazy mornings or afternoons either. So we'll get married in the winter and have lots of cold nights to laze in front of an open blaze in the fireplace in our bedroom."

"Are you sure, Lily? I'm just plain old Jesse Freeman who loves the dirt." He held her close.

"And I'm just Lily Winslow who thought she didn't like the dirt but made a mistake. It's where my roots and my heart are. Yes, Jesse, I'm sure," she said.

"Just one week and you are all mine," he said.

"Just one week and you are all mine," she teased as she hugged him tightly. "But for now you'd better get out of here or else we'd better go sit on the porch swing because . . ."

"Because you can't resist this old farmer, huh?"

"You *are* incorrigible," she giggled as she kicked back the covers and slipped her hand in his.

He drew her into his arms. He tilted her chin back with his callused palm and she could see that Jesse's eyes were smoldering. Not just twinkling or happy, but purely sensuous. Another side to the already complex sweet, old Jesse. Maybe when they were married fifty years she would know all the looks. But his hungry mouth found hers and she forgot about everything else when he slowly wrapped her warm robe around her and carried her out to the porch swing.

The snow had stopped falling and everything looked fresh and clean beneath the pale moonlight. Stars flickered in the sky like diamonds. And Lily didn't even think about the ring she'd thrown at Rachel that night so long ago.

"I love you, Lily. I've loved you since I first laid eyes on you," he whispered hoarsely as he strung kisses all over her face. He sat down in the swing and held her in his lap without even taking his lips from hers.

"Even that first day when I was sitting on the deck and you were all smelly and dirty?" She looked deep into his eyes and wrapped her arms around his neck even tighter.

"I just didn't know it then," he said.

"When did you know for sure, Jesse?" she asked.

"When I took you home to Coffeyville," he said. "I'd been fighting with it and I just gave in and admitted it that night," he said between long, lingering kisses that made her pant with desire.

"That's strange. That's when I knew I was in love with you, too. It was the most difficult thing I've ever had to do to watch you walk out that door. I thought I would die," she admitted, "But it won't happen again. I'm going to marry you and stay on this farm forever. No more separations."

"What kind of wedding can we get together in just a week?" he asked.

"I just want to be married to you, Jesse. It will be the simplest wedding in the whole world. If you'll be there with a plain gold wedding band, and not one of those big wide ones either. A little plain one like Aunt Molly wears . . . size six and a matching one for you.

I'll tell you where to go that afternoon. And please don't tell anyone we're getting married. I don't need family or anyone else. Just let them all think we're going to dinner. And, Jesse, wear your starched jeans and a white shirt. No tie, just that."

"Barefoot? In the middle of the winter?" He nuzzled her neck and she shivered.

"Dress boots," she said then forgot all about wedding plans as she kissed Jesse again . . . the only man in her mind, heart, or soul.

He had a faculty meeting that morning so she met him at the Dairy Queen in Tishomingo for lunch. She ordered a double bacon cheeseburger, fries, and a chocolate malt, and he told the waitress he'd have the same. "Some dinner for a wedding day," he said. "Besides, when Marcy got married, she couldn't see Jacob all day. They said it was bad luck if they saw each other."

"Not for us. We're special." She bit into the cheeseburger and rolled her eyes in appreciation. This was really living. Going to lunch with Jesse and eating like a field hand without him saying a word about fat grams and calories. Working beside him and then after tonight, crawling up into that big old four-poster bed with him. Heaven couldn't be any better than that. "Did you get our rings?"

"They're at the house," he said. "Laying on the bed right beside my shirt and jeans . . . and dress boots."

"Then eat up, honey, because tonight I'm staying at your house," she said.

"*Our* house, and *our* bed. The bed my grandparents slept in for sixty years. They bought it brand new and other than old lonesome me, were the only ones who ever slept in it. It was where my dad was born and maybe if things work out our son will sleep there someday," he held up his paper cup of Coke in a toast.

"Or our daughter." She clicked her cup with his, grateful that none of the other women in his life had ever slept in that bed. She might not be the first woman in his life, but she was sure enough going to be the last.

"Both. Lots of each." His eyes twinkled.

She took a simple pale blue silk dress from her garment bag. It matched her eyes beautifully and didn't have even a hint of white lace anywhere on it. She slipped into a pair of silky blue bikini underwear and a matching bra and then slipped the dress over her head and added a pair of light blue kid leather flat-soled shoes. She pulled her hair back into a french twist and let the ends make a topknot of curls into which she entwined a few silk forget-me-nots she bought at the flower shop. She was touching up her makeup when she heard the light tap at the door.

"Why did you knock?" She opened the door to find her handsome groom leaning against the frame with an appreciative smile on his sexy face, and Elvis sitting at the door beside his feet.

"If just a dinner date is important enough for a man to knock, then he should knock on his wedding day which is the most important day of his life." Jesse leaned forward and stole a kiss. "Momma and Dad have gone to some friends for the evening and Marcy and Jacob are at a party. We're all alone in the house so we don't even have to fabricate a story about where we are going all dressed up. Are we ready? My fate is in your hands from this moment on, since I don't know the plans."

"We're ready." She opened the door to let the cat out. "Go home, Elvis. We'll be back in a little while and I'll be there forever."

"You're truly beautiful. That's the same shade as your eyes." He fingered the soft fabric of the butterfly sleeves of her dress, touching her bare arm.

"Shhhh." She put her fingers over his lips. "You keep touching me and I'll forget my vows," she chuckled.

"Where to?" he asked.

"Why, where else but the store in Reagan where you first kissed me and I thought I heard fireworks," she said.

"I thought I heard bells from a train," he admitted honestly. "Are you sure you want to be married at that old place?"

"I'm sure. The preacher is meeting us there at six o'clock and we're getting married on the front porch. It's nippy out tonight but at least it's not snowing. Shouldn't take long and anyone comes up for business can just ignore us," she said.

Jesse laughed. "Marcy isn't going to believe it. What about witnesses? You just going to haul a couple of customers in for witnesses?" he asked.

"Never know." She kissed him quickly. "Let's go. The preacher will be waiting."

It didn't matter if she had told him to drive to the nearest two-hole outhouse or the biggest church in Ardmore, he would have gone gratefully. Lily was worth that much and more to him, and if she never wanted a piece of white lace in their house, then he'd see to it none crossed his doorstep.

He nosed the truck into the loose gravel on the south end of the store and walked around to open the door for his bride. She took his hand and stepped down and he was reminded of old western movies when men helped women out of horse-pulled wagons. They walked hand-in-hand down the length of the porch in front of the weathered store until they reached the two long wooden pews, aged by the blistering hot summer Oklahoma sun and the blue northers of winter.

The preacher sat at the end of one of the pews with his Bible in one hand and their marriage license in the other. Uncle Joe and Aunt Molly waited on the other pew. Jesse squeezed her hand and smiled. Lily had covered all the bases even better than he could have done.

"Evenin' Lily. Jesse? You two ready?" The preacher stood up. "Jesse, according to Lily's instructions, you're to stand right here beside these pansies and Mr. Joe is to stand beside you . . ."

". . . and I'm beside Lily." Aunt Molly wiped a tear away with a bright floral handkerchief. "I ain't been a bridesmaid in forty years, honey. And here's what you asked for. Something old, borrowed, and blue all in one old shawl. How's that?"

"It's absolutely wonderful and Aunt Molly, you're a beautiful bridesmaid." Lily slipped the warm shawl around her shoulders. Aunt Molly had a fresh rinse on her gray hair, turning it a faint shade of purple, and her navy-blue Sunday dress had been pressed until it didn't have a wrinkle in it. Uncle Joe wore his best pair of striped bibbed overalls and a blue and green plaid shirt and stood straight and tall beside Jesse with a serious look on his face.

"Dearly beloved, we are gathered here today to join this man and woman in the presence of these witnesses and God . . ." the Reverend started his shortest ceremony just like Lily asked.

Joe winked at Molly as they remembered the family reunion. Lily hardly heard the words as she listened to the song in her heart telling her she was the luckiest girl on earth, and if it hadn't been for the heartache Dylan put her through, she would have never met Jesse . . . or if she had, it would have been too late. Jesse said his vows, untraditional as they were, loud and clear while a middle-aged man filled his gas tank at the only pump in front of the store.

"I love you Lily, and I promise to be faithful to you forever. I want to share not only my natural possessions with you, but my heart and soul." He slipped the narrow gold band on her finger.

And Lily looked up at Jesse and repeated the vows of her heart as two teenagers parked their bicycles and went inside the store for a cold Coke. "Jesse, I love you and I promise to do everything I know to do to make you a good wife. I want to share my heart, my life, and our children with you," she said as she slipped the matching, simple ring on his finger.

"By the authority vested in me by the State of Oklahoma, I now pronounce you man and wife. Jesse, you may kiss your bride," the preacher said. And when Jesse kissed Lily . . . she heard fireworks in the distance and he heard a train whistle somewhere close by.

"I love you, Mrs. Freeman," he whispered as he hugged her close.

"And I love you, Jesse. Let's go home," she whispered back.

"Yes, ma'am." He tipped his hat back on his head, picked her up, and carried his new bride to the pickup truck.

Aunt Molly waved her rose floral hanky at them. "Keep the shawl for good luck. Maybe someday you'll wrap up a baby in it. Come see us when the honeymoon is over."

"Don't say that." Joe put his arm around her. "We'll never see them."

Lily called back over her shoulder, "See you in church Sunday if not before."

"Sure thing," Joe grinned and Molly slipped her arm through his.

Lily slid across the seat, wrapped her arms around her husband's neck, and pulled his mouth toward hers for another kiss, sealing their vows and future forever—on day one of a long and happy life together.